"*Vices?*" Raefe said scornfully.

"And what would you describe this as?" he continued. "Aboveboard and openhanded? *Honest?* To change your name and masquerade as someone you're not in order to worm your way into a household where you know damn well you're the last person who would be wanted?" The gray of Raefe's eyes resembled cold steel as he added, "And that brings us to *why* you did it."

The awkward question, of course, Francesca acknowledged, and paused before answering. It proved to be a fatal mistake.

Dear Reader,

A perfect nanny can be tough to find, but once you've found her, you'll love and treasure her forever. She's someone who'll not only look after the kids but could also be the loving mom they never knew. Or sometimes she's a he and is the daddy they are wishing for.

Here at Harlequin Presents® we've put together a compelling new series, NANNY WANTED!, in which some of our most popular authors create nannies whose talents extend way beyond taking care of the children! Each story will excite and delight you and make you wonder how any family could be complete without a nineties nanny.

Remember—nanny knows best when it comes to falling in love!

The Editors

Look out next month for:

A Daughter for Christmas
by Cathy Williams (#1993)

LINDSAY ARMSTRONG

Accidental Nanny

TORONTO • NEW YORK • LONDON
AMSTERDAM • PARIS • SYDNEY • HAMBURG
STOCKHOLM • ATHENS • TOKYO • MILAN • MADRID
PRAGUE • WARSAW • BUDAPEST • AUCKLAND

ISBN 0-373-11986-0

ACCIDENTAL NANNY

First North American Publication 1998.

Copyright © 1997 by Lindsay Armstrong.

CHAPTER ONE

SHE was about five feet six and in her early twenties, he judged, with a fine carriage that displayed a slender neck, straight shoulders and breasts that bounced beneath the yellow silk of her shirt like tantalising fruit as she jumped out of a dusty Land Rover. Her waist was small, her hips compact, her legs, in blue jeans, long. She also had an imperious air and glorious toffee-coloured hair. Then she spoke, and there was absolute assurance in her cultured vowels—the inborn ease of someone who had been used to having all and sundry do her bidding from her cradle...

Raefe Stevensen narrowed his eyes then raised a wry eyebrow. So it's true, he mused. She has been up on Wirra. He paused and watched the girl toss her head as she spoke to the man who had driven her. I can guess why she's here—and expecting me to drop everything, no doubt. He watched a moment longer, then deliberately reached for the telephone.

Francesca Valentine jumped down from a battered Land Rover and looked around intently. There was not a lot to see—one prefabricated building, a hangar, one runway with a limp airsock, two light planes and a helicopter parked on the apron. Her deep blue eyes brightened at the sight of the aircraft, however, and she turned to the driver of the Land Rover, flicking her toffee-coloured hair back. 'This'll do, Jim. You don't need to wait around. You'll be wanting to get back to the station before the road is flooded anyway.'

'Well…' The driver, a dusty, middle-aged man, hesitated. 'I don't like to leave you, Miss Valentine. Your father—'

'Jim, so long as there are planes, I can get myself flown out.'

'But just in case you can't,' Jim persisted. 'This is a very small town, Miss Valentine. There's only one pub where you could stay and you wouldn't—well, it's not what you're used to. Cattlemen, drovers, *truckies* and the like,' he added with deep significance. 'Your father—'

'If you mention my father once again, Jim, I'll scream. It was his idea that I spend some time on Wirra Station; therefore, even if indirectly, it's his fault that I'm all but stranded here!'

'He couldn't have organised this flood,' Jim replied reasonably. 'And it wasn't his fault the chopper conked out on us at a time like this.'

'Don't you believe it,' Francesca said darkly, but added, 'Look, surely it's easier for you not to have me to worry about on top of everything else? I mean, you're going to have enough on your plate as it is, what with moving stock around let alone yourselves if the waters get up to the homestead.'

Jim sighed and said cautiously, 'We could be cut off for weeks, I guess.'

'Exactly! The other thing is, once I get home, I can pull all sorts of strings towards getting you parts flown

up to repair the helicopter,' Francesca finished trium-
phantly.

'OK, Miss Valentine, if you say so,' Jim relented
suddenly, and got out to heave her bag off the back
seat. 'I'll just carry this to the office for you.'

'I can do it.' Francesca wrested her bag from him
and held out her hand. 'Goodbye, Jim. I do appreciate
your concern, and I hope I wasn't too much of
a...time-waster for you. I shall certainly report back
that Wirra is in good hands.'

'Cheerio, Miss Valentine. As for being a time-
waster—well, I doubt if those lads have enjoyed themselves as much for years once they got used
to...certain things, so don't you worry your pretty
head about it.' As he shook her hand vigorously he
appraised not only her pretty head but also her shapely
figure with a genuine and kindly appreciation that gave
no offence. 'You're a right card at times, Miss
Valentine,' he added. 'A real chip off the old block—
and it's been a pleasure.'

'Not too much of a chip, I hope,' Francesca murmured, but beneath her breath, and then she stayed to
wave Jim off before turning once more to survey the
landscape of this tiny airfield in the middle of North
Queensland's Cape York Peninsula.

The rain depression that had blown in off the Gulf
of Carpentaria had not yet hit, although the sky was
heavy. But the floodwaters generated by the depression were creeping inexorably down the channels and
river beds and, according to all predictions, it wouldn't
be long before this wild country that was home to
some huge cattle stations would not only be awash

from those creeping waters but deluged by the skies above. The northern part of Wirra Station was already under water.

Wirra, Francesca mused, and thought back briefly over the last two weeks that she'd spent on the newest acquisition of the diverse, powerful and immensely wealthy Valentine empire.

There had certainly been a tangible restraint amongst most of the employees towards the new owner's daughter at first. And if it hadn't been for Jim, whom she'd known for years and who'd been transferred from another Valentine property to take over the running of Wirra, it might have been quite uncomfortable. But with his help I managed to win them over, I think, she reflected. Am I really a chip off the old block? I know Dad can be immensely charismatic when he sets his mind to it, but there's a hard, cold side to him I hope I haven't inherited…

'Oh, well,' she said aloud, and turned towards the small building that proclaimed from a sign on the roof that it was the home of Banyo Air—the three craft on the tarmac bore the same logo. 'The sooner I get myself out of here the better!'

It was an unimpressive office she walked into, with one girl behind a battered desk, two uncomfortable orange plastic chairs in front of it and a view through grimy windows of the airfield. There was a watercooler, a sluggish ceiling fan churning the hot, humid air and a variety of blown-up aerial photos tacked to the walls. Francesca dumped her bag down and said crisply, 'I'd like to see whoever is in charge, please.'

The girl, who looked no more than nineteen, blinked

and pushed her dark hair back nervously. 'He's on the phone at the moment—' she gestured to an inner doorway behind Francesca '—but if you'd care to wait he shouldn't be too long.'

'What's his name?'

The girl blinked again. 'Stevensen. Mr. Stevensen,' she said finally.

'Then perhaps you can help me, if Mr Stevensen is too busy. I need a flight to Brisbane—'

'Brisbane?' the girl echoed, her eyes widening, as if the capital of Queensland were located on the moon.

'Yes, well,' Francesca said, reflecting that Brisbane *was* over a thousand miles away. 'Cairns, then, or at least somewhere where I can get a regular flight. You do fly to Cairns?'

'We could,' the girl said cautiously, 'but I'm afraid I couldn't arrange anything like that.'

'Then would you mind letting this Mr Stevensen know that I am here?'

'Yes. As soon as he finishes his call,' the girl amended. 'Would you like to sit down, or perhaps you'd like a glass of water?'

'Both,' Francesca said with a grin, and helped herself to a paper cup.

The girl seemed to relax, and she spent a few moments covertly admiring Francesca—her designer jeans and silk shirt, for one thing, and her soft kid tan boots. She gazed at her narrow, elegant hands, and the one ring she wore—an unusual gold signet on her little finger—and the way her toffee hair fell to her shoulders in a beautifully ordered, shining mane. Then she sighed discreetly and picked up the phone.

Francesca listened idly, because there was no point in trying not to, and discovered that the girl was talking to the Acme Employment Agency in Cairns with a view to hiring a governess for the unseen Mr Stevensen's motherless seven-year-old daughter. It further transpired that his sister, who usually looked after the girl, had broken her wrist and that the job would entail living on a cattle station.

'Yes,' the girl said into the phone, 'Bramble Downs, that's right. Yes, it is a bit isolated, although it's *very* comfortable. But no, no shops handy—no cinemas, no libraries, no television or anything like that—and it can get very hot...'

Not to mention flooded out—why don't you tell them that? Francesca thought with a grimace but did not say. And when the call was ended, and there was nothing else to do as the girl began to bang away at an old typewriter, she pondered on the difficulty of getting staff to these remote areas and found herself wishing Mr Stevensen luck in the matter of a governess for his motherless seven-year-old daughter.

Then she glanced at her watch and discovered that she'd been waiting for twenty minutes, and her goodwill towards the elusive man began to seep away. Another five minutes, she told herself. How busy can he be in this God-forsaken spot?

She waited for precisely five minutes, then she stood up and said politely to the girl, 'What is your name?'

'Susan— Look, I am sorry, but he's still on the phone, although I'm sure he knows you're here. He would have seen you arrive.'

'Is that so—Susan?' Francesca said precisely.

'Well, will you take this message in to your boss? Will you tell him that Francesca Valentine, daughter of Frank Valentine—yes, that one, the multimillionaire,' she said as Susan's eyes bulged, 'would like to see him immediately? Furthermore, will you tell him that if he keeps me waiting any longer I will buy out this tinpot little airline he works for and have him *sacked*?'

Predictably, Susan couldn't find the words to respond, but it was a moment before Francesca realised that she might not be the whole cause of the girl's distress. Because Susan was in fact staring fixedly at a point over her right shoulder, and she swung on her heel to discover that the inner door must have opened silently during her speech and now a man stood there.

For once in her life Francesca herself was rendered speechless, although only momentarily, because the elusive Mr Stevensen—if this was he—was not what she'd expected at all. What had she expected? she was to wonder later. Had the unpretentious, grimy office with its poor facilities led her to expect the same of the man in charge? Had the locality, which wasn't that far from the black stump, led her to expect a slowly-spoken cattleman-type, who would blink in awe at her?

How wrong could you be? she was also to think later, because this man was certainly not blinking in awe at her. He was eyeing her narrowly and insolently. He was over six feet tall, with fair hair and grey eyes, and he was in his middle thirties, she judged. And as well as being good-looking, and well although casually dressed, in khaki trousers and shirt, he carried an unmistakable aura of *savoir-faire* directly alongside the aura of a tough and hard man.

Francesca took an unexpected breath, but opened her mouth immediately. 'Well, well, is it you at last, Mr Stevensen? To what do I owe this honour, or have I got the wrong man?'

'I am Raefe Stevensen, and if you wish to be flown out of here, Francesca Valentine, daughter of Frank Valentine, I'd advise you not to take that tone with me.'

'How dare you—?' Francesca began.

'I dare for several reasons,' Raefe Stevensen said in cool, even tones that barely cloaked the contempt beneath them. 'You can't buy me out because I own this airline. You won't find any other way to get to Cairns today. And, last but not least, your father's millions mean nothing to me—I can't stand the man.'

Francesca's nostrils flared and a steady little flame lit her blue eyes. 'Then may I say that I'm sure the feeling would be mutual—if this is the sloppy way you run a business.' She flicked a scornful hand.

'And may *I* say that your thoughts on the subject, or any subject, are quite without interest to me, Miss Valentine.'

'Is that so? Well—'

But he overrode her casually. 'You don't know what you're talking about, and—' that cool, insolent grey gaze swept up and down her body '—you look about as glamorous and useless as the spoilt little rich girl you are. Why don't you go away and find someone else to terrorise? I'm not flying you to Cairns today.'

'Oh, yes, you are, mate,' Francesca said through her teeth. 'I'll pay you…whatever you want—you name it. And, on the subject of how useless I am, I've just spent the last fortnight on Wirra, doing most of the things all the men did—'

'Yes, I heard about that.' Raefe Stevensen smiled unpleasantly. 'But being good on a horse and a motorbike doesn't mean to say you're any good at anything else. The other interesting item of news on the bush telegraph was that you'd been banished up to Wirra by your father for some rather sordid indiscretion down south.' He leant back against the doorframe, folded his arms and studied her mockingly. 'It's a pity to be the subject of that kind of gossip at—what—twenty-two?'

A white-hot gust of anger visited Francesca, and she stepped right up to Raefe Stevensen with every intention of slapping his face. But, although he moved lazily, he managed to grasp her wrist with one hand and with the other like an iron bar around the back of her waist bent her backwards over it.

Sheer surprise held Francesca transfixed for a second. Then she squirmed vigorously, only to have herself clamped ruthlessly against a body that was as hard and strong as a tree-trunk. She was also unexpectedly assailed by a curious sensation of helplessness and, to her horror, an undoubted awareness of all that was masculinely attractive about Raefe Stevensen.

And in the brief moment before he lowered his head to kiss her she saw, to her further horror, in those cool grey eyes that *he* was all too aware of the effect he was having on her.

It didn't take long, his kiss, but it contrived to be comprehensive and merciless. 'There,' he drawled as he released her and politely steadied her, adding insult to injury, before dropping his hands from her body. 'Is that what you wanted, Chessie Valentine? I believe that's what those in the know call you, and I suppose I could be considered "in the know" now.' His lips quirked. 'Sorry it couldn't have been a bit more intimate, but we do have company.'

Francesca stared up into those supremely ironic grey eyes, blinked several times in disbelief then turned to see Susan watching them with all the pop-eyed intensity of a trapped rabbit. She swung back to Raefe Stevensen; the pause had given her a little time to compose herself.

She said grimly, 'I'm afraid you got it wrong, Mr Stevensen, sir, and—'

'You're about to tell me I'll pay for this somehow or other?' he suggested. 'Will you report me to Daddy?'

What shook Francesca as much as anything that had happened to her was that his words were said with the unmistakable indifference of a man who really did not care—a man who believed she was an indulged, *useless* millionaire's daughter, if not worse.

Did I ask for it? The thought popped into her head, taking her unawares. I know I can go over the top sometimes, but to keep *anyone* waiting for nearly half an hour when you're only in the office next door— surely that wasn't necessary! It's not as if he owns Ansett or Qantas. But how the hell am I going to get away from here now?

'You were saying?' Raefe Stevensen prompted.

Francesca opened her mouth, closed it, then said stiffly, 'If I overreacted to being kept waiting for what seemed—I have to be honest—an inordinately long time, I apologise.'

'Go on,' he murmured.

'On? What more do you want me to say?'

'I was wondering how you might try to cajole me into flying you out.'

Francesca closed her eyes and cautioned herself to stay cool. 'Well…' She paused, then shrugged. 'You have the option of flying me out to Cairns at the going rate, Mr Stevensen, or not. It's up to you.'

'And if I don't?'

'Then it sounds like a night at the pub for me until I can arrange something else—because if you think I intend to grovel at your feet,' Francesca said softly, 'you're wrong.'

'Not the pub.' Susan spoke for the first time in a fairly desperate, bewildered sort of way. 'I mean, it's full of stranded truck drivers and tourists. *Raefe,*' she added on an anxious, entreating note, and glanced at Francesca.

For the first time Raefe Stevensen's grey eyes softened as they rested on the girl's face. 'Sorry, Susie,' he said. 'That was a bit rough on you. Uh…call Bill, will you? He's in the hangar and he's scheduled to take the Beechcraft down to Cairns this afternoon. Tell him to leave as soon as he can.'

'Rough on you,' Francesca heard herself repeating somewhat dazedly, and added, 'I think I must be going

round the bend! I mean, I'm sorry too, Susie, but—'
She broke off and shook her head disbelievingly.

'It's all right, Miss Valentine,' Susan said hastily.

Whereupon Raefe Stevensen grinned and murmured, 'It seems you have one fan, Chessie, despite your high-handed ways.'

'Don't call me that,' Francesca warned grimly. 'How would you like to be paid? I have a credit card, or—'

'I'm sure you have the lot,' he drawled.

Francesca, in the act of opening her purse, which did indeed hold an impressive array of credit cards, paused, then tossed her head and laid the open purse down on the desk. 'You're quite right. Take your pick, Mr Stevensen.'

'Well, Chessie Valentine, I think I might give you this one on the house,' he said. 'The plane was going to Cairns anyway, and one more piece of—baggage— is not going to make any difference. You should be able to take off within an hour. Good day to you— I'm about to fly off myself. I don't suppose we'll meet again, which might be a good thing. Should be back in a couple of hours, Susie.' And he strolled out of the office without a backward glance.

Francesca barely restrained herself from picking up her purse and flinging it at his retreating back.

She put up at the luxurious Cairns International that night, after finding herself unexpectedly exhausted, although the flight by Banyo Air to Cairns had been uneventful.

But the next morning she woke to find herself in a different mood altogether. She got up early, showered, wrapped herself in a cool, silky robe and ordered breakfast. While she was eating a delicious mango she knew she should be getting on to one of the commercial airlines to fly her south, but in fact she couldn't tear her mind from the events of the previous day, and the humiliation she'd suffered at the hands of one Raefe Stevensen.

What surprised her, though, was the fact that she was possessed of almost equal desires not only to avenge herself but to prove him wrong. Why? she wondered. A lot of people out there assume I'm a rich bitch. It comes with the territory—especially when you have a father like mine...

She flinched, and got up to examine the view from her window. But no view of Cairns could distract her from the truth, which was that, after her mother's death when she was six, her father had taken a series of mistresses—some nice, some ghastly—and the only shield between herself and them had been years at an exclusive boarding-school. Years of yearning for a normal family life until she'd grown a protective shell that was both brittle and bright and sometimes outrageous.

I know it, she thought. I know I can be impossible, and I suppose it's really ironic that when I am impossible I emulate the very worst side of my father, who I basically despise, but that's not all there is to me.

Still...she grimaced...I must have acquired more of a reputation for being a chip off the old block than I realised, and I certainly must have acquired more of a reputation for being a dilettante, not to mention glamorous but *useless*, than I realised if people buried in the wilds of Far North Queensland have heard about me.

Mind you, she countered to herself, I can't be held responsible for the fact that the reason I came to be at Wirra got wildly distorted, and why should I care what one insufferably arrogant man thinks of me?

She returned to the breakfast table with the uncomfortable knowledge that she *did* care, even if she couldn't understand why. Her hands stilled as she started to butter a piece of toast, and a gleam came to her blue eyes. Now, Chessie, don't rush into this, she told herself, but a few moments later she reached for the phone to call Reception and advise them that she required a fax machine. Then she made several calls to Melbourne, her home town—only one of them being to do with the parts required for the malfunctioning Wirra helicopter.

An hour later the faxes started to roll in satisfactorily. Two hours later she dressed carefully in her most conservative clothes.

She chose cream linen trousers, a cream and green checked blouse and polished brown moccasins. She tied her rich hair back demurely with a green ribbon and she wore no jewellery other than her signet ring and a man's plain watch with a leather band. She applied no make-up.

She folded her faxes carefully and tucked them into her shoulder bag. She then took the lift to the foyer where the head porter, with sweeping bows, procured a taxi for her and directed it to the offices of the Acme Employment Agency.

'I believe,' she said to the lady behind the desk at Acme, 'that there is a governess position available at

Bramble Downs—the Stevensen family. I happened to hear about it and, since I have teaching qualifications and I'm on a working holiday in this part of the world, I thought of applying for it.'

The woman, whose name-tag labelled her as Joyce Cotton, blinked, then smote her forehead. 'Glory be! I was getting quite desperate! Poor Mrs Ellery has broken her wrist, and as if that isn't bad enough she's just rung me to say the cook's gone walkabout. She really needs help urgently now, but they have very high standards and it's just not that easy to find quality staff—or any kind of staff,' she added honestly, 'for these stations.

'Then there are floods up there, I believe, so Raefe Stevensen—he's the girl's father—is going to be desperately busy and can't be home. Mind you, I'll have to check you out before I can—'

'Of course,' Francesca said, and just thinking of Raefe Stevensen and the way he'd kept her waiting with no sign of being desperately busy, let alone the way he'd kissed her, helped her to say without a twinge, 'My name is Fran Moorehouse, and I've brought along copies of my references and so on. You're welcome to check them out.'

Not that I'm really telling a lie, she mused, having been christened Francesca Moorehouse Valentine— Moorehouse was her mother's maiden name. And Fran Moorehouse was a name she often used to escape notice.

To do Joyce Cotton credit, she diligently checked most of them by phone, then said, 'Right, Fran, I think that will do. Now there's only the problem of getting you up there. What a pity it's not yesterday! Raefe had a plane land in Cairns, I believe, but anyway, I'll get on to him straight away. You can—'

'Joyce,' Francesca interrupted, 'where exactly is Bramble Downs? I'll tell you why I'm asking: I have a four-wheel drive, and if it's at all possible to drive myself up there I'd rather do that than have to find somewhere to leave it.'

Joyce Cotton frowned, then pulled out a large-scale map. 'It's at *least* a six-hour drive from here, Fran, on difficult roads. And then there are the floods—but they may not have reached... Look, I don't know about this,' she finished anxiously. 'On the other hand, if it saved Raefe a trip...'

Francesca studied the map and noted that Bramble Downs was on the east coast of the peninsula and about two hundred miles south of the town and airstrip she'd flown from yesterday. 'Could...?' She paused and frowned. 'Perhaps I could get a road report from the RACQ? They should have up-to-date information.'

Joyce brightened and reached for the phone. It transpired that Bramble Downs should be accessible until the following afternoon at least.

'Well—' Francesca smiled '—that solves that.'

'And you have no qualms about driving up there on your own?' Joyce enquired.

'None,' Francesca assured her.

'You know,' Joyce said warmly, 'I think you're just the practical, capable kind of person the Stevensens need!'

'Thank you,' Francesca responded, with what she

hoped was hidden irony, and ten minutes later she
stepped out into the bright sunshine.

She then applied herself to the task of acquiring a
four-wheel-drive vehicle at extremely short notice, and
also all she would require for a stay of unknown du-
ration on Bramble Downs.

CHAPTER TWO

TEN days later Sarah Ellery, Raefe's sister, who was in her late thirties, said, 'Fran, I don't know how on earth I coped without you! This wretched wrist.' She waved the offending arm with its plaster. 'You just don't realise how difficult it is to manage one-handed. I can't believe the good luck that brought you our way. Raefe will be so delighted when he gets home—which should be any day now.'

Francesca hid a grimace. The floods had subsided, and although Bramble had been cut off for several days they hadn't received nearly the inundation that had affected areas further north. The same inundation that had kept Raefe Stevensen from home as Banyo Air was heavily involved not only in moving people about to escape the waters but also in mustering half-drowned stock. All of which couldn't have suited her plans better.

But Judgement Day had to come, and, while her resolve stood firm concerning the man, his family was becoming another matter.

She glanced across to where young Jess Stevensen was doing a jigsaw puzzle, with the tip of her little pink tongue sticking out as she concentrated fiercely. She was a fair, serious child, and at first she'd shown an almost adult reserve that had puzzled Francesca slightly. But the reserve was lessening day by day—

in fact she was beginning to show flashes of sweetness and affection that were quite beguiling.

Then there was Sarah, thin and elegant, with her brother's eyes, although darker hair, and a gold wedding ring on her finger but no sign or mention of a husband. Sarah, who'd also been reserved at the start, and had a hint of unexplained sadness about her—although she too had dropped her guard after a couple of days and shown that she possessed a delightful sense of humour as well as being cultured and artistic. She read avidly, painted lovely miniatures and played the grand piano beautifully. Even one-handed.

Indeed, the whole of the Bramble Downs homestead had come as something of a surprise to Francesca. Its facilities alone were impressive, considering how far away from anywhere they were, and represented the considerable amount of money that must have been spent to achieve the degree of comfort there was on a property that had no town water or electricity.

Then there was the house itself. Solid and comfortable, it was in a magical position overlooking a white beach, an island and reef-studded waters that changed colour from aquamarine to dark blue depending on the time of day and tide.

It was surrounded by lawn and smothered in bougainvillea, and its thick white walls, cool tiled floors, wide verandas and Spanish-flavoured interior suited the tropical climate perfectly—it could not have been more different from the virtually tin-shed accommodation on Wirra, and it was obvious the Stevensen family was not short of cash.

Some demon of curiosity had prompted Francesca to ask Sarah one day whether Jess's mother had been responsible for the uncluttered interior, the lovely pieces of heavy wooden furniture and the occasional splash of colour in a rug or a painting or a giant pottery urn filled with dried flowers.

This had provoked a brief, sad look from Sarah, although no explanation of what had actually happened to Jess's mother, before she'd composed herself and replied that no, not really, it had mostly been her and Raefe's mother's doing. Then she'd gone on rather deliberately to chat about the family history, and Francesca had got the distinct impression that the subject of Jess's mother was taboo.

But she had discovered that Bramble Downs had been in the Stevensen family for eighty years. It had been taken up by Sarah's grandfather, and the original residence had been nothing but a tin shed. Now, whilst cattle had always been and still was the largest part of their business, Banyo Air, started by Raefe, was growing most satisfactorily. It was obvious to Francesca that Sarah Ellery was very fond of her brother.

'He was always fascinated by flying, although he's a cattleman through and through,' Sarah added dreamily, then grinned wryly. 'He even used to try to construct wings. I remember the day he jumped off the water tank and broke his leg. And he couldn't wait to get into the Air Force. He was one of their top guns,' she said proudly.

'Is that all he did?' Francesca heard herself ask,

and hoped the slightly cynical note she heard wasn't obvious to Sarah.

Sarah blinked and said, 'Well, he did some sort of aeronautical engineering degree at the same time as he trained to be a pilot. Then he left the Air Force and did a stint for a year as a private pilot for some sheikh. Now that was quite an experience. The man had four wives and fourteen concubines, would you believe, and he used to jet around the world as we might drive into town.'

'It must be quite a change—I mean from that to running Banyo Air,' Francesca said casually, and at the same time she thought, so that accounts for the *savoir-faire*.

'But, you see, he's his own boss now and Banyo Air is acquiring quite a reputation—it's actually the perfect combination for a cattleman, especially now that so much mustering is done by helicopter. He has the experience of cattle—he was inducted into that almost before he could walk—he knows the peninsula and the gulf really well, and he's a first-class flier. So contract mustering is the mainstay of Banyo Air, but he also runs scenic charter flights and so on.'

Francesca thought of the trim craft she'd flown in to Cairns, and indeed of the disparity between all the polished craft that had stood upon the apron that fateful day and the unprepossessing offices of Banyo Air. Her thoughts were tinged with bitterness—if the offices had been as trim and polished as the aircraft Raefe Stevensen flew, might she have been more restrained herself? So why *did* he operate out of a tin-

pot sort of office if Banyo Air was so highly regarded?

Sarah answered that right on cue. 'His next project
is upgrading the facilities at the airport he operates
out of. It's badly needed, believe me. But these things
take time and money. And planning permission,' she
added with a grimace.

Francesca pondered all this anew as she was getting
ready for bed that night. Her bedroom with its *en
suite* bathroom was comfortable and pretty, with a
double bed, a cool tiled floor and yellow sherbet coloured curtains and bedspread. She had a dressing table and a writing table, both made from silky oak,
and one comfortable armchair, and it was into this
she sank to examine, with a rather strange feeling,
how well she'd slipped into the lifestyle of Bramble
Downs.

Not only had she taken Jess over from the head
stockman's wife, who had been helping Sarah out
since she'd broken her wrist, but the cook's disap-
pearance had given her the opportunity to exercise
her culinary skills. All of which had meant she'd had
hardly a minute to herself, yet she felt curiously ful-
filled and satisfied.

And, more than that, it was as if she was saying to
Raefe Stevensen, yes, I can see that the way the Valentine millions are flaunted and the way I acted that
day would be an affront to someone who comes from
this quiet but solid, achieving and cultured background of yours—but you still misread me!

The one thing she couldn't do was visualise his
reaction to her presence at Bramble, although she told

herself that he surely wouldn't react too excessively in front of his sister and child. What she didn't count on was that their first meeting would take place without anyone to witness it...

She woke just before dawn the next morning and listened to the birds saluting the new day for a few minutes—birds you didn't hear down south, and ones that would always be inextricably linked in her mind with Far North Queensland, with its heat, its isolation, the thick mat of turf beneath your feet as you stepped off the veranda at Bramble, with the casuarinas and pandanus palms that rimmed the beach and the lovely waters of the Great Barrier Reef...

Just thinking of it prompted her to take the opportunity, while Jess still slept, to go for a dawn swim. She pulled on a violet bikini, brushed her hair, reached for a towel and slipped out of the house noiselessly as the first rays of light touched the sky.

Because of the proliferation of crocodiles in this part of the world since they'd become a protected species, as well as the prevalence of the deadly box jellyfish in summer, a wire-mesh and pole swimming enclosure had been built which extended into the water and up the beach. Francesca clicked open the gate, saw that the tide was high, which meant plenty of water to swim in, and ran down the beach to dive in.

It was heavenly—still cool enough to be refreshing, salty and with a gentle swell that lifted her rhythmically off her feet. After she'd swum up and down energetically for about ten minutes, she lay in the shallows and watched the sun rise in a symphony of apricot and lemon as the birds sang on. Then she heard the enclosure gate click open and, thinking it might be Jess, sighed lightly and stood up to start her daily duties.

But it wasn't Jess, it was the girl's father, with his shirt and shoes already off and his hands frozen on the waistband of his khaki trousers.

Francesca froze too, and they stared at each other over about six feet of sand, close enough for her to see the disbelief and then the sheer, deadly anger that came to his grey eyes, the way all the muscles of his strong, streamlined torso and arms bunched and the knuckles of his hands went white.

It crossed her mind with a genuine tremor of fear that she might be about to come to an early demise on this beautiful beach so far away from anywhere, but then his eyes changed to unreadable, those muscles relaxed and he unclamped his jaw to say roughly, 'Fran something or other? What a fool I was not to connect the name when Sarah rang me about the gem of a new governess they'd sent her. How did you do it, *Francesca* Valentine? Forge a few references? Or did you buy out Acme?'

The savage scorn and disgust in his voice seared Francesca and she went a little pale. But she managed to say evenly, 'I forged nothing. I—'

'Oh, come on! How the hell do you expect me to believe that?'

'I don't care what you *choose* to believe,' she said tautly. 'But you won't be able to disbelieve that I have an arts degree with a teaching diploma because I can prove it. I can also prove that I've worked regularly with handicapped children, and those institutions were very happy to supply me with references.'

'What about your honesty and integrity?' he shot back.

'Strangely enough, I had no trouble finding several people to vouch for my honesty and integrity—people who were even happy to commit to paper the fact that I had no police record, no vices, no—'

'Vices?' he said scornfully. 'And what would you describe this as? Above-board and open-handed? *Honest?* To change your name and masquerade as someone you're not in order to worm your way into a household where you know damn well you're the last person who would be wanted?' The grey of his eyes resembled cold steel as he added, 'And that brings us to *why* you did it.'

The awkward question, of course, Francesca acknowledged in her mind, and paused before answering to make sure she presented her case coolly and clinically. It proved to be a fatal pause.

Raefe Stevensen advanced several steps to stand right in front of her and look down at her with all his old insolent cynicism as he said softly, 'Don't try to con me further, *Chessie*. I know the answer. You don't like to think any man can walk away from you, do you? You came here with one aim in mind, *didn't* you? To add me to your list of scalps.'

There was so much tension between them that Francesca found herself briefly possessed of the notion that the air was crackling with static, and she realised as she spoke that her voice was alive with it. 'Don't you kid yourself, Raefe Stevensen,' she said unevenly, barely concealing the wild anger that ran through her veins.

But he only looked coldly amused. Then he subjected her damp, glowing body to the most minute scrutiny. Her bare neck and shoulders, her firm lovely breasts and the erect nipples clearly visible beneath the wisp of violet silk, the curve of her hips and thighs, adorned by what suddenly seemed to Francesca to be a particularly small triangle of silk, the sweep of her legs. He scrutinised her so effectively, she was made to feel as if he was running his hands over every curve, every secret, intimate part of her.

Then he said mockingly, 'This is really why, isn't it, Chessie Valentine? You can't believe any man could be unaffected by your...' his grey gaze swept her body again '...admittedly very beautiful body, your lovely face and, most of all, your father's millions. You assume that they will distract them from your shallow little soul.'

Francesca stared at him with her lips parted incredulously.

'And that's why,' he went on, 'you're to be found on *my* beach in your designer bikini. I'm quite sure if this hadn't happened first you'd have found the opportunity to parade yourself before me in it somehow,' he finished with lethal gentleness.

Francesca came to life, bent to gather her towel and forced herself to tie it around her waist steadily, although her fingers were trembling, and only when she was done did she say, 'If you ever insult me again, Raefe Stevensen, or take it upon yourself to kiss me again, believe me, you will pay—even if I have to use all of my father's despised resources to achieve it. Now get out of my way,' she ordered.

But he laughed softly, and then really took her breath way. 'It's no crime to look. Why don't you come for a swim with me? Perhaps I could send you away from Bramble not entirely—frustrated.'

And he moved around her, dropped his trousers carelessly to the sand and strode into the water.

Francesca had barely reached the safety of her room and started to toss clothes into her bags when she heard, through her window, Sarah say delightedly, 'Why, Raefe! When did you get home? *How* did you get home? Gosh, you're all wet!'

Francesca clenched her fists then moved to the window so that she could see out of it but was hidden by the yellow sherbet coloured curtain. She was just in time to see Raefe bestow a light kiss on his sister's brow. He'd put his trousers on but his fair hair was plastered to his head and dripping and his tanned, magnificent shoulders glistened with droplets of water in the early sun.

She heard him say, 'I've only just arrived. I drove down because all the choppers are out. For the last fifty miles all I've been thinking of is a swim.'

Sarah laughed. 'Good thinking! No one's up yet. Raefe, you wouldn't believe how lucky we are with the new governess! She's even got Jess to sleep in—and she cooks too!'

'Does she, now?' Raefe Stevensen said on a distinctly dry note, but his sister seemed not to notice.

'I'm just hoping and praying she'll stay with us. But I do wonder…'

'What do you wonder, beloved?'

'Well, she's—I'm sure she's capable of doing much more with her life, somehow. She's very well educated, and from the odd thing she's let slip she's well travelled and so on… By the way, did I mention she's absolutely lovely as well?' Was there a touch of ingenuousness in the way Sarah said that? Francesca wondered.

'You did not—I can't wait to meet this paragon. Why, if it isn't Miss Jessica Stevensen!' he added, and fielded a joyful, flying, fair-haired missile, sweeping her up into his arms. 'How are you today, poppet?'

'I'm fine, Daddy,' Jess replied excitedly. 'Guess what? I've got a new governess. She says I can call her Chessie and she's teaching me to do long division.'

'Goodness me—won't be long before I'll be able to hand the books over to you, but—'

'I really like Chessie,' Jess went on. 'She's also teaching me to swim—'

'You *can* swim,' her father objected.

'But I'm learning to do backstroke now,' Jess said proudly.

'I see.' Raefe put her down but kept her by his side as his long fingers played with her fair curls. 'Uh— would you tell this Chessie I'd like to see her in my study in half an hour, please?'

'She'll be starting breakfast by now—why don't you see her in the kitchen, Raefe?' Sarah suggested.

'By the way, don't forget I have to get to Cairns somehow tomorrow for an X-ray to see how my wrist is healing.

'You know, I thought, seeing as you're not so busy now, and seeing as Fran—or Chessie—is here and coping so admirably, I might just take a bit of a break. I haven't been to Brisbane for a while.' Sarah stopped, and it was as if a cloud had gone over the landscape of her expression for a moment. 'But I really should go,' she added quietly. 'What do you think?'

Francesca moved away from the window with a suddenly thoughtful frown.

'We meet again, Miss Valentine.'

'So we do, Mr Stevensen.'

'Sit down.'

It was about an hour later. Francesca had made and served breakfast, although not to Raefe, who had not appeared in the kitchen but sent a message to keep his hot. She had also packed her bags and was dressed in her cream trousers and cream and green checked shirt. Sarah had taken Jess for a walk, fortuitously, so the house was empty, and Francesca had taken the bull by the horns and walked into Raefe's study. She sank into a chair.

They eyed each other until he said casually, 'I thought you'd have shaken the dust of Bramble from your shoes by now, Chessie. I presume that brand-new four-wheel-drive vehicle is yours?'

'It is—I had no intention of being at your mercy again over the matter of transport,' she replied crisply, then added abruptly, 'How do you want to do this?'

'Do what?' He'd changed into navy shorts and a white T-shirt, and the task of driving two hundred miles overnight appeared not to have made any impact on him as he lounged behind the beautiful mahogany table that served as a desk.

'As if you didn't know—arrange my departure,' she said scornfully. 'Because I refuse to simply disappear. I don't do that to children, or people I happen to like.'

He sat up and clasped his hands on the desk. 'What do you suggest, Chessie?'

Francesca reined in her anger at the insulting way he used her name. Everything was insulting to her, including the way his grey gaze lingered on the front of her checked blouse, as if he was seeing beneath it. 'I could claim to have had a call to go home for some urgent reason. That way I can say goodbye properly.'

He appeared to reflect for a moment, then said, 'We still haven't got to the bottom of why you did this—want to tell me?'

'Oh, I thought we had,' she replied innocently. 'You seem to have worked it out down to the last dotting of the i's and crossing of the t's!'

'I gather you have another version, though.' There was a glimmer of amusement in his eyes.

'Ah, but why waste my time, since you're so determined to disbelieve anything I say?' she murmured with irony, and added, 'Look, let's get this sorted out, shall we? I'd like to get back to Cairns by tonight.'

'Chessie...' He frowned, then sat back. 'What

would *you* believe of a girl who is frequently seen on the social pages in revealing gowns and with rent-a-crowd escorts? Whose twenty-first birthday party was a three-day event on Hayman Island? Who was given a Porsche for her eighteenth birthday? Whose name has been linked romantically with a lot of men and who, apparently, was banished up to this neck of the woods by her father because of an involvement with a married man?'

Francesca blinked. 'Who told you *that*?'

'It's not true?' he countered coolly.

'No, it's not! Not in that sense—I wasn't *banished*. If you think my father can afford to moralise to *me*—' She stopped abruptly.

'Go on—so there was no married man?'

Francesca stared at him, then said wearily, 'Yes, there was, but, believe me, it was he who was making a nuisance of himself, not the other way around.'

Their gazes locked and held, and Francesca's deep blue eyes did not waver. Nor did they hide her sense of outrage.

This caused Raefe Stevensen to smile briefly and say, 'So why did you do this?'

'For the sheer pleasure of proving to you that I am not *useless*,' she said proudly.

He raised an eyebrow. 'I must have hit quite a nerve.'

'And I presume it would be too much to expect for you to admit that you may have made a mistake about me, but it doesn't matter,' she said swiftly, and stood up. 'As they say in Asia, I hope you have an interesting life, Mr Stevensen. Your brand of arrogance certainly deserves it!'

But he only laughed softly. 'Chessie,' he remonstrated, still grinning, 'you have a very short memory! Are you not the girl who started all this by threatening to buy out my means of livelihood and have me sacked? If that's not arrogance...' He shook his head wryly.

Francesca clenched her fists, and he watched with interest the effort she made not to take the bait. 'Look, I'm *going*,' she said. 'I'll tell them whatever I please, and—'

He interrupted her to say, 'I've got another idea. Why don't you stay for a couple of weeks?'

'Oh, no. Oh, no! How can you *possibly*—?'

'Perhaps we could start again,' he said smoothly.

'Start again? You've got to be joking.' Her glance was withering.

'No, I'm not.'

'And neither am I. You seem to forget that all I did was take exception to being kept waiting for so long—the first utterly arrogant action in this duel if you ask me—'

'I was on the phone,' he said mildly.

'And you surely don't believe what *I* said was anything more than a retaliatory tactic?' she shot back. 'Whilst *you*...you insulted me, kissed me against my will and this morning took the unbelievable liberty of—of undressing me with your eyes, which is to put it very mildly. No. And don't bother to offer to pay me either, Mr. Stevensen. This—*baggage*—would rather you owed her one.' She turned on her heel.

'There wasn't a lot of you left to undress,' he said. 'But—I apologise for that.'

Francesca looked over her shoulder. 'Only that? Oh, well, I didn't think you had it in you to do even that. It won't get you anywhere, though. Good day to—'

'I apologise for the rest of it, then. Perhaps I did rather overreact.'

Francesca paused, then swung around. 'You must rate me as really cheap, Mr Stevensen,' she said gently. 'That won't do it either.'

'All right, Chessie.' He narrowed his eyes. 'What would do it?'

'Nothing that I can think of—so you might as well get right on to Joyce Cotton at Acme, although I must tell you she was at her wits' end until I turned up.'

She watched and waited, and saw his frown deepen as he studied her. Then he said abruptly, 'Look, it so happens I really need you for the next couple of weeks. And, since it would appear that you have been both an excellent governess and cook, I would be much obliged if you would help me out. I take back the "useless" tag unreservedly.'

Francesca was silent for a moment, because she wasn't sure that she believed him entirely, nor was she altogether sure whether she should be doing what she was doing. Then she discovered that she still had a few things to prove to Raefe Stevensen.

'OK, I'll do it. For two weeks.'

'I thought you might,' he said drily.

'What do you mean?' She blinked.

'You heard Sarah this morning, didn't you? It's

just occurred to me we had that conversation on the lawn virtually outside your window. And, accordingly, you knew I'd be fairly desperate. I'm only surprised you didn't ask me to grovel at your feet.'

A faint tinge of colour came to Francesca's cheeks but she didn't deny the charge. 'Yes, I heard. And, yes, I decided to milk as much of an apology out of you as I could. You're welcome to sack me for it.'

'Why?' he said simply.

She looked at him steadily. 'Are we back to that? Because I still have some things to prove to you, Mr Stevensen. And one of them is that when I do walk away from Bramble your—scalp or whatever you like to call it won't be attached to my belt.'

'That's a very rash statement, Chessie,' he murmured.

'Just wait and see.'

He considered for a moment, then said with a faint shrug and a wry little look, 'Aren't you at all afraid of the opposite happening?'

'Opposite to what?'

'Well, in light of my "unbelievable liberties", quote unquote, mightn't I have designs on *your* scalp?'

'You know, I almost wish you would,' she said thoughtfully, and there was a sudden glint of contempt in her eyes. 'For the sheer pleasure of knocking you back as well as proving to you that you're no better than the rest of them, despite the high moral tone you've taken with me. But in fact you'll have to content yourself with this—one hint of any further liberties, even in anger, and I will leave you and your daughter high and dry.'

He gazed at her, then smiled suddenly. 'It should be an interesting fortnight—but I give you my word; if you're happy to leave *me* alone in that... er...direction, I shall be only too happy to do the same for you.'

The glint in Francesca's eyes changed from contempt to anger, but Jess and Sarah came into the study at that point. And Raefe stood up to say, 'Well, we've got Chessie for a while longer, at least, so why don't you plan your trip to Brisbane, Sarah?'

CHAPTER THREE

'I HOPE you don't feel as if I'm—imposing,' Sarah said that afternoon. Francesca was helping her to pack and Raefe had taken Jess for a drive to inspect stock and fences.

'Why should I think that?'

Sarah gazed at her. 'I just thought I detected a slight restraint in you.'

Francesca bent over the suitcase on the floor and laid a linen skirt neatly in it. 'She'll be fine with me, I *promise* you.'

'It's strange,' Sarah said after a moment, 'but I've got the feeling I know you, Fran. I've had it since we first met—silly, of course, because I've racked my brains and I know we haven't ever met.'

Francesca sat back on her heels, pushed her toffee hair back and considered. Then she said, 'You've probably seen me on what your brother so scathingly calls the "social pages".' She turned to Sarah and added levelly, 'I'm afraid I've misled you.' And she told Raefe's sister the bare bones of how she'd come to be at Bramble Downs.

Sarah sat transfixed for half a minute as it all sank in, then she said in an awed voice, 'You didn't—I mean, you did, obviously, but how brave!'

Francesca grimaced. 'Not so much brave—I have an awful temper, and impossibly high-handed ways at times—but what really annoyed me was his assumption that I was a glamorous but useless and spoilt little rich girl.'

Sarah blinked.

'Perhaps I shouldn't have told you—if it's going to worry you,' Francesca said after a pause. 'But I'll tell Jess my real name and I do promise I'll take great care of her, I won't let it affect her.'

Sarah came to life. 'I'm quite sure Raefe wouldn't do anything to affect her adversely either—she's so precious to him. No, I'm consumed with admiration. Raefe's got such a mind of his own—has had since he was a baby,' she said wryly.

'You're not wrong,' Francesca agreed drily.

'You'll probably find he admires you underneath it all,' Sarah suggested after a moment's thought.

Francesca stood up and smiled down at this sometimes sad woman she'd come to like a lot. 'I wouldn't bank on it.'

'But—that is what you've set out to prove, more or less, isn't it?'

Francesca had turned away, and was glad she had because Sarah's words unearthed a strange feeling at the pit of her stomach. But she managed to say slowly, 'Not to make him like me, if that's what you mean—I don't think we could ever see eye to eye as much as that. It's just...' She stopped and sighed suddenly.

'It's not that easy to avoid publicity with a high-profile name like mine. A lot of it is speculation—although, I have to admit, there are times when my...' she hesitated '...temperament leads me into falling into traps of my own making. But—oh, well...' She shrugged.

'And people, particularly men, can be quite dense sometimes, can't they?' Sarah said sombrely.

Francesca grimaced. 'They're certainly quite prone to believing the worst of me.'

She turned back to Sarah and they suddenly exchanged smiles of understanding that gave Francesca an oddly warm feeling.

Early the following morning a helicopter from Banyo Air landed on the lawn and Sarah left for Cairns and eventually Brisbane. Raefe, Francesca and Jess waved her off.

It was Francesca who noticed that Jess, as the little craft rose, hovered then flew away like a noisy bird, seemed to droop.

'Why don't we go for a swim?' she said casually. 'We can try some more backstroke—and don't forget I promised to build you the biggest sandcastle in the *world* today!'

Jess brightened immediately, and Raefe Stevensen said, 'Yes, why don't we?'

Francesca turned to him abruptly with her nostrils pinched, her mouth set in a grim line, but Jess was so obviously delighted to have her father along as well that she turned away immediately and schooled herself to behave as normally as possible.

She would have been even more annoyed, although not entirely surprised, had she been able to read his mind. Because Raefe Stevensen was watching her taut back at the same time as he found himself thinking, nearly got you there, Chessie Valentine—it's not going to be as easy as you think, is it, my beautiful termagant? I wonder how many men you *have* driven out of their minds with your wilful ways and that gorgeous body?

'I can do it! I can do it!' Jess sang excitedly, then stopped and sank as she swallowed a mouthful of water.

Raefe brought her up, spluttering. 'The trick is probably not to talk while you're doing it—don't you agree, Chessie?'

Francesca nodded, and did some backstroke herself while Raefe patiently took his daughter through the motions again. The water was like pale blue glass as it stretched away to the horizon, and the sky was the same blue, while the air was starting to shimmer with heat. It should have been a pleasant experience, this swim, she mused, before the fierce power of the sun turned the water tepid. But she felt uncomfortable and tense.

Mindful of what had happened to her the previous morning, she'd put on a one-piece buttercup-yellow swimsuit—and been on the receiving end of a wickedly raised eyebrow for her pains. But, of course, the difficulty of it all was that she'd virtually given herself as a hostage to this man since making the promise she had to his sister, and not only that—she wouldn't upset Jess, anyway—but why hadn't she stopped to consider all the implications?

Now look here, Chessie, she reminded herself as she floated on her back, isn't that exactly what you set out to prove? That you could remain quite unaffected by him? So why this faltering at the first fence?

She twisted over suddenly and dived beneath the surface. When she came up, it was to see that Jess and Raefe were wading through the shallows to the beach, and it all came clear to her.

There was, much as she'd like to think otherwise, an undeniable frisson between her and Raefe Stevensen. The kind of frisson that was going to make it hard for her to leave the sea with water streaming off her body and the buttercup Lycra moulding every curve of her figure—hard, that was, beneath those cool, sometimes derisive eyes.

Because she had no doubt he would be watching her, and no doubt that, whatever he might think of her shallow mind and her father's millions, her body was not a matter of complete indifference to him. Nor, perhaps more unfortunately, were the clean, strong lines of him quite lost on her, and she knew that it would not be possible to deny the trickle of awareness that would run through her as a result of it all as she walked up the beach.

Damn, she thought. I must be mad! Why *did* I do this? How right was he?

It was this thought that steadied her. Because he hadn't been right about her; she wasn't a collector of scalps. And just recalling his words made her stiffen her spine, swim to where she could find a footing and stride out of the water with what she hoped was the appearance of complete indifference.

'There. Big enough?' Raefe said to Jess.

Francesca had covered herself with a white cotton shirt and a wide-brimmed straw hat by this time. Jess always wore a specially protective swimshirt over her togs to minimise the effect of the sun on her fair skin, and a floppy white hat, but Raefe was bare-shouldered and hatless as he worked away at the sandcastle.

He sat back and admired his handiwork—the castle was almost as tall as his daughter. He'd done most of the digging while Francesca and Jess had shaped it and adorned it with stones, little wild flowers gathered from the grassy verge beside the beach, and boat-shaped leaves to float in the moat that surrounded it.

'What we need is a flag,' Francesca murmured. 'Tell you what—it's really getting a bit hot out here now, so why don't we go in and do a bit of school-work and make a flag?'

'Yes. Yes!' Jess jumped up and down enthusiastically. 'But—' her eyes widened '—what happens when the tide comes in? Will it still be here?'

'Ah,' her father said. 'Good point. But you've got at least four or five hours, because the tide's going out now. You know...' he looked around with a frown '...for years I've been meaning to build a sun shelter on the beach.'

'And you were also going to build a barbecue here,' Jess reminded him gravely, and laid a small, sandy hand on his cheek.

For some reason, Francesca saw Raefe Stevensen take a sudden breath as he gazed at the little girl. And for some equally unexplained reason he then raised his eyes to Francesca, and they were as cold as steel.

She blinked, but the moment had disappeared and he was saying wryly to Jess, 'You're so right, Miss Muffet. OK, I'll start doing something about it today.

Over to you, Miss Valentine,' he added expression-lessly.

Francesca hesitated, but he got up and strolled down the beach, obviously intent on picking a site for his sun shelter and barbecue. And although Jess seemed to notice nothing amiss it was, to Francesca, an un-necessarily abrupt dismissal. But she shrugged and took Jess's hand and they went up to the house to-gether.

Part of the wide, screened veranda that led off Jess's bedroom had roll-down blinds to keep out the sun, as well as sliding windows, and had also been furnished as a playroom and schoolroom in one.

There was a two-storeyed, fully furnished dolls' house, quite old by the look of it, but well made, and Jess adored it and played with it for hours, and there was a rocking horse, an array of teddy bears in all sizes, two golliwogs, six dolls, a pram, a giraffe that was taller than Jess and a menagerie of smaller toy animals.

A lot of them looked as if they'd been handed down from a previous generation, but that didn't disturb Jess. She had names for them all, she conducted con-versations with them and often held tea-parties for them.

Francesca had been both amazed and touched at Jess's vivid imagination as she managed her family of toys. It was mostly the golliwogs who caused a lot of the mischief, apparently, although there were days when the teddies got out of hand and had to be se-verely reprimanded. There was also one particularly naughty monkey, with a bright red waistcoat and a bell on his hat, who caused Jess to shake her fair curly head in despair at times. His name was Mo.

'If he's good,' Jess said that morning as they sat down at the schoolroom end of the area, with Mo hanging from the back of a chair by his tail, 'I'll take him down to the sandcastle and let him help us plant the flag. What do you think, Chessie?'

'A good idea,' Francesca said seriously. 'Has he been bad lately?'

Jess considered. 'No, not *too* bad. I think he gets lonely. If he had another monkey friend it might help.'

'You could be right—although if he's anything like those two gollies over there it could make him worse. But you never know; it's worth a try. Now, let me think—perhaps we could make him one?'

Jess clapped her hands, then sobered. 'But how?'

Francesca thought for a bit. 'We'd need some furry material.' She picked up Mo and studied him, then smiled. 'And if we made a girl monkey we could call her Flo! We might be better off with a girl; she might be a better influence on him.'

Jess was enchanted, and remembered that Sarah had a sewing machine and a bag full of all sorts of scraps of material.

'Well, we'll have a look this afternoon. In the meantime let's have another go at these long division sums, then we'll read a bit more.'

The morning passed, and a paper flag was made and coloured in then planted in the sandcastle with Mo's help. After a simple lunch of cold meat and salad that they ate on their own, Francesca and Jess followed a time-honoured custom in the fierce heat of the middle of the day—they had a rest. Raefe had apparently gone out on cattle business.

Sarah's sewing machine was set up in the laundry that adjoined the kitchen, and by a piece of good luck— for Francesca had begun to wonder how on earth she was going to come up with some furry material in this part of the world—her bag had yielded what looked like the remains of the synthetic fur lining of an overcoat, as well as colourful scraps to make clothes and enough rags with which to stuff Flo. There was also a sewing box, with buttons et cetera, and they spent a pleasurable afternoon constructing a new monkey.

'There,' Francesca said at about five o'clock. 'Nearly done! I've got to start dinner, Jess, but I'll put the finishing touches to Miss Flo Stevensen tonight— now don't tell Mo about her; we'll give him a surprise tomorrow!'

As she finished speaking Francesca felt a prickle of awareness, and turned to find Raefe standing at the kitchen door watching them. Jess immediately ran to him, full of excited explanations about the new monkey. He picked her up, his eyes curiously intent on her flushed, happy little face, then looked across at Francesca.

For some reason—whether it was to do with her willing participation in Jess's imaginary world or her flash of revelation about the effect he had on her earlier in the day she wasn't sure—she felt her cheeks grow warm.

Raefe put Jess down and said gravely, 'I'm sure you'll find Mo quite a reformed character, Jess. I'll look after her until dinner is ready,' he added to Francesca, and took his daughter off.

Bramble Downs homestead was too remote to be connected to the state's electricity grid, but there were two generators that dispensed power and light, and another two down at what was really the heart of the station, about two miles away—the head stockman's cottage, other staff cottages and the cattle yards.

Having spent two weeks on Wirra, which had a similar set-up, Francesca had got used to the constant hum in the background, and since taking over the cooking at Bramble she actually gave thanks for it, because the kitchen was equipped with all mod cons and she didn't have to battle with a wood-fired stove. But it occurred to her as she went into the kitchen and reached for an apron that it would strike not only her father but also her friends as bizarre, to say the least, if they could see her now.

Not that they weren't used to her doing the odd bizarre thing, such as the time she'd crewed on a yacht in the Sydney to Hobart race—the only girl in the crew—and the weeks she'd spent in Sarawak and Sabah once, getting to know the orang-utans. No, her being at Bramble Downs in itself would raise no eyebrows. But if they were to see her acting as the paid governess and cook, taking orders from a man who, moreover, patently despised her, they would surely wonder whether she was sickening for something.

She grimaced as this thought brought her up short. Sickening for something? What? No, not that. Certainly not *love* sick, although a bit of healthy lust might be another matter. Dear me, she mused, you'd better watch it, Francesca Moorehouse Valentine—and was interrupted in these uncomfortable musings by the head stockman's daughter.

Annette Brown, daughter of Bob and Barbara Brown, was just eighteen and an apprentice hairdresser in Cairns. She was home at the moment, on a short holiday, and she often helped her mother out with the cleaning and the laundry at Bramble homestead.

'Brought the ironing up, Fran,' Annette said as she dumped a laundry basket on the counter. 'And Mum sent a couple of fresh-baked loaves.'

Francesca received the two golden crusty loaves gratefully. One thing she did not do successfully was bake bread. 'Your mum is a darling, Annette. Please say thanks very much.'

Annette parked herself on a kitchen stool. She had a lively rather than pretty face, and she was a bright, straightforward, down-to-earth teenager. 'How's it going?' she enquired of Francesca. She was deeply interested in everything about the new governess.

'Pretty good.' Francesca took some veal steaks out of the fridge and assembled breadcrumbs, mustard, Worcestershire sauce, an egg and some milk. 'Jess doesn't seem to be missing Sarah so far, but I guess it's a help having her father around.'

'She loves Raefe madly,' Annette agreed. 'But then that's not hard to do.'

Francesca raised an enquiring eyebrow.

'Had a bit of a crush on him myself once,' Annette said airily. 'Of course I never *showed* it, although I think Mum guessed.'

'Well, I'm glad to hear you got over it.'

Annette produced a packet of chewing gum, offered Fran a piece, which she declined, then started to chew vigorously. 'Men can be tricky, Fran, can't they?'

'Er—oh, they can.' Francesca beat the egg and milk and poured the breadcrumbs into a dish. Then she started to brush mustard onto the veal and sprinkle it with Worcestershire sauce. 'Not Raefe, though?' she added with a frown.

'No!' Annette smiled ruefully. 'If he thinks of me at all he probably thinks I'm still eleven or twelve. No, what I wanted to ask you, Fran—seeing as you're a bit older and you look kinda sophisticated—is this. How can you know you're going to enjoy sleeping with a man until you actually do it?'

'Well, Annette, I'm afraid I can't help you there,' Francesca said, torn between amusement and the need to say the right thing. 'I've not actually done it myself yet, you see.'

'What?' Annette's eyes popped. 'But you must be *years* older than I am!'

'Thank you,' Francesca said politely. 'About five, actually. I'm twenty-three, and while I've certainly come close to it a couple of times I...' She paused, just stopping herself from saying, I've never been completely sure it was me, not my father's money they wanted, and said instead, 'I don't think I've ever been in love enough.'

'So you reckon...' Annette chewed thoughtfully '...it's a good idea to wait?'

'Yes, I do,' Francesca said definitely, and added as an afterthought, 'Is there someone you...?'

'Yeah. We met at a bush dance. His name is Jericho,

would you believe? I mean, I couldn't stop laughing when he told me. You'd think you'd just call yourself Jerry if you had a name like that, but he's not one for doing that. He doesn't duck out of things, if you know what I mean. He's also got the biggest feet I've ever seen.'

'And he's asked you to sleep with him?'

'No. But I can't work out what I would do if he did—I can see he's got it on his mind at times.'

'How old is he?'

'Twenty. He's a fitter and turner, when he's not playing rugby league.' Annette raised her eyes heavenwards. 'Actually, he wanted us to go away together this holiday, but I wasn't too sure about it. I guess, though, now I know about you, I'll wait until I'm at least twenty-three before I do anything like that. Hey, thanks, Fran—and listen, don't forget, if you want your hair done, or if there's anything I can do at all, just give me a call!' She slid off the stool and departed cheerfully.

Leaving Francesca staring after her and strangely unsure whether to laugh or cry.

'What I need is a bell!'

'A bell?' Raefe Stevensen repeated, coming into the lounge where Francesca sat on a settee putting the final touches to Flo. It was about nine o'clock. Jess had been peacefully asleep for a couple of hours and her father, up until now, closeted in his study. 'A school bell?'

'No. A bell like the one Mo has on his hat.' She held Flo up for his inspection.

Instead of glancing at it idly, Raefe took it out of

her hand and studied it quizzically. 'Now that's quite a feat,' he remarked, handing it back to her and walking across to the cocktail cabinet. 'How come you're so domesticated, Miss Valentine? Like a nightcap, by the way?'

Francesca considered. 'I wouldn't mind a brandy and soda if you've got it.'

He had it, and went into the kitchen to get some ice to go with it. Ice that clinked against the cut-glass Stuart crystal tumbler he handed her.

'Thanks,' she murmured, and added, 'To what do I owe this honour, Mr Stevensen?'

He poured his own drink, then turned to study her thoughtfully before sitting down in a comfortable armchair opposite her.

She'd changed for dinner into a light, airy, pale blue dress with a round neck and cap sleeves, loose and waistless so that it floated around her when she moved. With it she wore blue sandals that exactly matched her dress and which consisted of slender straps over the front of her feet, no backs and small wedge heels. She'd pulled her heavy hair back at the sides and secured it with combs. The pale blue of the dress and shoes highlighted her smooth, tanned limbs.

He said at last, as she watched him with growing enquiry in her eyes, 'Is it such an honour, Chessie?'

'Considering how little you like me, I would imagine so.'

'And that's something you plan to change, is it?'

'No.' A smile curved her mouth. 'Sorry. You see, the very last thing I would like to hear you say is "I told you so, Chessie"!'

'You think I would?'

'I'm sure you would.'

He laid his head back and studied the ceiling for a moment. 'So you thought this was a prelude to…' He paused, lifted his head and squinted at his glass wryly. 'To getting myself into the position where I would be able to say that to you?'

'It crossed my mind.' Her blue gaze rested on him with some amusement.

'And you don't have any qualms about being alone in a house miles from anywhere with someone about whom you cherish those suspicions?'

'You mean am I worried that you're going to leap on me and rape me? No, I'm not. Not in front of Jess. But of course there's always seduction,' she went on cheerfully.

'You say that…' he paused again to look at her rather intently '…as if that holds absolutely no fears for you either.'

She smiled. 'When you've had as much experience in being the object of attempted seduction as I have, Raefe—may I call you that?—you can see it coming for *miles*.'

'What about love? Has that ever happened to you?'

'I've thought so a couple of times, but it proved to be the same old thing.'

He raised an eyebrow. 'So you weren't very adept at distinguishing between love and seduction—at least a couple of times?'

'*Touché,*' she responded, a shade drily. 'I won't have that problem with you, though, will I? I mean, should the undoubted physical awareness we share ever show signs of getting out of hand, I'll always know it's not love, won't I?'

He took his time, staring at her openly but enigmatically before he replied. When he did it was to say musingly, 'I'm not sure if you're a straight-shooter, Chessie Valentine, or—' his lips twisted '—the absolute opposite.'

'Don't I know it—I have to wonder the same about you, amongst other things.' She shrugged casually.

'All right,' he said abruptly, and set down his half-finished drink. 'I'd have to be a block of wood not to be impressed by you in certain respects. I hope that makes you happy. But I have also to tell you I have no intention of doing anything about it.'

Francesca considered. 'That's fine with me, as a matter of fact,' she responded at last, and put down her own drink to stand up. 'Because, while I believe in being honest, I have also to tell *you* that I'm just as contemptuous of purely physical attractions as you are. You don't *own* the moral high ground, Mr Stevensen, and it might be a good idea if you remembered that. Goodnight.' She walked out, taking Flo with her.

Raefe Stevensen watched the way the pale blue material swirled around her long legs, how it fell against her supple figure, how she held her head as if she had the whole world at her feet. And he picked up his drink to finish it in one long swallow. Then he examined the empty glass with a frown and thought, how could she possibly be for real? How the hell could Frank Valentine's daughter be...?

He put the glass down impatiently, stood up and

went to a cabinet, locked but with the key in it. He
turned it soundlessly. He took out a silver-framed
photo and stared down at the features behind the glass,
remembering how Jess had laid a hand on his cheek
earlier in the day and reminded him so much of
Olivia... He clamped his teeth together, hard, and put
the picture away.

CHAPTER FOUR

To say that an armed truce existed for the next few days would have been to state the case accurately.

Raefe, with the help of Annette's father, Bob Brown, the head stockman, began to construct the beach shelter and barbecue. This time of the year, as Francesca had come to be instructed, was generally known as the 'wet', and was a fairly slack time for cattle stations. A time when the staff was cut to skeleton proportions because no serious mustering of cattle was done, and a time when those staff remaining worked on maintenance of fences, cattle yards, equipment and so on.

It seemed that Raefe was leaving Banyo Air to run itself at the moment as well, or at least he wasn't involved in such a hands-on way as before. And he spent as much time as possible with Jess, taking her out and about with him around the property—expeditions Francesca was not invited on.

She caught herself feeling slightly chagrined about this, because she would have loved the opportunity to compare Bramble with Wirra—the amount of stock they carried and so on—and because she was acquiring a fondness for the wild country of Cape York, with its pink, sandy earth tones, its deep ochre bauxite rocks, its white beaches and magnificent seascapes.

She was also—and this struck her as something to

57

be wary of—revelling at times in the lifestyle the Stevensens had carved out for themselves in the wilderness. The lack of television didn't bother her in the slightest. There was an extensive library and there was the piano, which she didn't play as well as Sarah but played well enough to enjoy herself and be able to give Jess some lessons, and there was plenty to do inside the house and out of it.

She would have dearly liked to do some gardening—something she'd never done in her life before but found strangely alluring—and there were times when she would have loved to jump on a horse or a motorbike and really exert herself checking fences, bores and pumps, and all the other things she'd learnt to do on Wirra. But even without this it was curiously satisfying to go to bed at night knowing she'd contributed some small bit to the well-being of Bramble.

Except, that was, on those occasions when she'd been left behind, and she forced herself to be honest about that and admit that, on top of all else, she simply felt left out...

As for Raefe, during those days he was scrupulously polite but unmistakably distant.

It's quite possible he doesn't altogether trust me with Jess, Francesca thought once, and shrugged. But the truth was she and Jess were getting along like a house on fire, and the little girl seemed unaware of the constraint between her father and her governess. Mind you, Francesca thought, why should Jess expect any different? She drew her brows together. Am I imagining it or do I detect that Raefe Stevensen doesn't altogether like the closeness that has grown between us? And *why* is there never any mention of his wife?

She pondered this with another frown, remembering the day Sarah had almost tangibly drawn a curtain over that topic. There were also no photos of anyone who might conceivably have been his wife, and Jess never mentioned her mother. If she had died, surely some reminders of her would have been kept? If she had run off with another man—well, perhaps not. Could it be, in consequence, that Raefe Stevensen was not utterly cynical on the subject of Francesca Valentine alone— but about the whole tribe of women?

Four days after their confrontation in the lounge, she was to discover not only that he *did* resent her closeness to his daughter, but also why.

It all started out innocently on a rainy day—although that was a mild term. It poured all day and had poured all night. This effectively put a stop to the work on the beach shelter, which apparently now only required the finishing touches—and just as effectively brought the three of them into each other's company. But while Francesca and Jess were able to occupy themselves happily with a mixture of schoolwork and play, by mid-afternoon Raefe was prowling around the house like a caged tiger.

'Daddy doesn't like having nothing to do,' Jess confided.

'I can see that.'

'Well, I thought I'd clean out my dolls' house—is that a good idea, Chessie?'

'I think it's a brilliant idea. Rainy days are great days for house-cleaning. Do you need a hand?'

'No, thank you,' Jess said importantly. 'I'm going to rearrange *all* the furniture. *If* those gollies don't worry the life out of me.'

'I could take them into the kitchen with me. I thought I'd make some chocolate-chip biscuits. How is Mo these days, by the way?'

Jess glanced affectionately at Mo and Flo, who hung side by side from the bookcase. 'Just what Daddy said he would be. Quite re…?'

'Reformed,' Francesca supplied.

'I think you were right, too—it's all because Flo is a girl.'

Francesca grinned and took the two golliwogs with her to the kitchen where she sat them side by side on the counter and warned, 'Just behave, you two!'

'Or you'll…?' Raefe said from the doorway.

She swung round ruefully. 'It must be catching.'

'I guess it must,' he drawled, and strolled over to pull a chair out from the kitchen table. He turned it around and sat astride it with his arms propped along the back. 'I was wondering whether you were going to threaten them with being turned into girls, or perhaps you're planning to construct mates for them?'

'You heard it all,' Francesca said after a moment, and glanced at him narrowly. Because she had an odd little feeling that he hadn't enjoyed what he'd overheard.

'I heard it all,' he agreed, then said abruptly, 'Do you think she lives too much in this make-believe world?'

'I—well…' Francesca said cautiously as she got out

the flour et cetera. 'She's an only child, and she's only seven—'

'But in your experience of seven-year-olds?'

Francesca paused and stared at the package of chocolate chips in her hand. 'I have no real experience of so-called "normal" seven-year-olds,' she said at last.

'But you told me you were a teacher.'

'I said I had an arts degree with a teaching diploma, but I haven't actually taught.'

'I don't know why, but that doesn't surprise me in the slightest.' His grey gaze was mocking.

Francesca put the chocolate chips down carefully. 'Well, I know why it doesn't surprise you—you'd be simply devastated if I wasn't totally as black as you've painted me, Mr Stevensen.'

'I thought we'd got to Raefe?'

'You thought wrong. That was an aberration,' she said shortly.

'So how come you did a teaching diploma with no intention of teaching?'

'I had a very strong-minded headmistress, if you must know. She took the view that nothing was incapable of changing, not even the Valentine millions, and that in any case it was a waste of one's talents to spend one's life being a spoilt little rich girl. She was also responsible for sending me to a cordon bleu cooking school, and she forced me to take a dressmaking and sewing course.'

He raised an eyebrow. 'So that explains that.' He watched her sifting flour then rubbing butter into it. 'But you must have disappointed her somewhat, Chessie. You don't teach, I would imagine the time you spend with handicapped children is not exactly a career and, forgive me for doubting you, I'd be most amazed if you'd sewed any of the clothes I've seen you wear...'

He looked at her in amusement, but it was entirely at her expense, and pointedly took in the long pearly grey skirt she was wearing with a white cotton bustier top. Both articles were light, casual and comfortable, perfect for the heavy humidity that lay upon the air like a warm blanket, but there was no denying that they were exquisitely styled and made from the finest materials.

There was also no denying that she wasn't wearing a bra, although the top was perfectly proper in that it was not see-through. But his gaze lingered on the satiny tanned skin of her throat and shoulders, and the dew of perspiration that was starting to run down between her breasts.

Francesca controlled the urge to throw something at him. 'As a matter of fact—and this may have escaped your notice—I *am* my father's sole heir to date, so I'm being groomed to take over from him.'

'It's rather strange that he didn't remarry, isn't it?'

'It's none of your business,' Francesca said sharply, and bludgeoned the biscuit mix into a long roll on the floured board. 'Now look what you've made me do,' she added exasperatedly.

He raised an innocent eyebrow.

'I forgot to put the chocolate chips in!' She formed her hands into fists, so as not to transfer the mixture to her skirt, and put them on her hips.

'Sorry—perhaps you could just decorate the biscuits with them? Stick them on top, in other words.'

She didn't deign to reply, but started to cut the roll neatly.

'You're a bit sensitive on the subject of your father, aren't you?' he mused after a while. 'Not that I blame you.'

Francesca stopped cutting. 'Very. So be warned, Mr Stevensen. In fact don't say another word on the subject.'

He eyed the long knife in her hand and his lips twisted. 'As you say, Miss Valentine. Is that why you were up at Wirra? Other than escaping the unwanted attentions of a married man, I mean. To learn about the Valentine empire?'

'Yes.' Francesca lowered the knife, although her eyes still glinted with anger. 'And if you must know I wouldn't mind seeing a bit of the Bramble operation, so I could compare the two, but I gather that is an honour I'm to be denied.'

'And for a very good reason, Chessie,' he said softly. 'Well, two,' he amended.

She blinked.

'I'm not in the habit of giving the opposition guided tours of my properties, for one thing—particularly not the kind of opposition who acquired Wirra dishonourably, as your father did.'

Francesca gasped. 'He did no such thing!'

'Oh, yes, he did,' Raefe countered coolly. 'You see, I happen to know the previous owner of Wirra Station, and I happen to know that he was persuaded to part with it for a song—at least a third less than its true value and more likely half.'

Francesca stared at him. 'So that's it—I mean, I don't know anything about the actual purchase of Wirra, although I do know that precise values are not finite things, but *that's* why you hate the very sight of me!'

He smiled drily. 'I thought we'd established that we aren't actually averse to the sight of each other, Chessie. You made that point a couple of nights ago, rather forcefully. I—'

'Stop,' she commanded. 'Don't think you can throw me off the track by indulging in sexual innuendo. I want to know precisely what happened with Wirra!'

'All right,' he drawled. 'The previous owner was in debt to one of your father's companies. Now, I firmly believe a debt is a debt, but this *was* a drought-induced debt and the honourable thing would have been for your father either to allow the previous owner to sell Wirra at the best price he could get for it and then meet his obligations or, since the drought had broken, let him work the debt off over a couple of good seasons.

'He didn't do that. He insisted on negotiating a deal whereby he acquired Wirra dirt-cheap and my friend was forced to walk away from it with virtually nothing.'

Francesca realised her mouth was open, and closed it with a click. Then she took a deep breath and said with dignity, 'I apologise—'

'You're not going to deny it?' Raefe said mildly.

'I can't. Not that I knew anything about it, but I do

know my father can be a very hard businessman. Also...' she paused and looked unseeingly at the golliwogs '...it makes sense of some of the remarks I overheard when I first arrived at Wirra—and some of the restraint, I guess. I now see why the Valentine name was not the most highly regarded—I suppose most of the staff were from the previous era?'

Raefe nodded. 'But you changed all that, I gather?'

Francesca subjected him to a proud, deep blue gaze. 'What are you implying?'

'I'm implying that two weeks of Chessie Valentine doing her stuff on horses and motorbikes et cetera would certainly have helped win them over. And did you swim while you were up there? Well, we know *I'm* not a block of wood, so why should we expect it of some simple, women-starved bush cowboys?' he said lazily.

Her cheeks reddened but she refused to allow her temper to take over, although it left her quivering with effort. 'You said there were two.'

'Two?'

'Two *reasons*,' she ground out. 'Why I'm not to be shown anything of Bramble.'

'Ah.' He stood up and pushed the chair back neatly under the table. 'Yes. I don't think it's a good thing for Jess to get too fond of you, Chessie. Or to come to regard you as an integral part of her lifestyle— you're only going to be here for another week or so, after all. And if you've conceived the idea that the way to get through to me is via Jess, perish the thought, my dear. I'm quite aware of it, you see.'

* * *

'These biscuits don't have any chocolate chips,' Jess commented at afternoon tea.

'I know. I forgot to put them in—or on,' Francesca replied. 'Silly me.'

'Never mind,' Jess consoled her. 'It must be the weather.'

Francesca stared through the wire netting to where the rain was teeming down and obscuring the view, and she lifted her heavy hair off her neck after a moment, a little helplessly. 'It must be.'

But it stopped raining after dinner, when she was putting Jess to bed, and a light breeze got up that was sheer heaven.

When Francesca was sure Jess was properly asleep, she anointed herself with mosquito repellent, got a torch and went for a walk. Mosquitoes and sandflies, as well as crocodiles and box jellyfish, were a fact of life in this part of the world, and you either learnt to live with them and took precautions or went mad, Francesca suspected as the lawn squelched underfoot.

And it was rather ruefully that she turned the torch off when she came to the beach, because it was attracting all sorts of other insects that fluttered against her skin, giving her the shivers, or dive-bombed her hair.

Paradise? she mused. Not entirely. As for Raefe Stevensen...

She sat down on a smooth, flat rock and watched the faint line of fluorescence that marked the waterline on the beach and listened, with a curiously empty mind, to the gentle lapping of the wavelets. I'm lost, she thought eventually. Whichever key I turn, it's only to have the door slammed in my face. Even the care I've taken of his child has rebounded on me...

She put her hand out to touch the rock next to the one she was sitting on and was surprised to find it warm and curiously scaly. Then it moved and she leapt up, switching the torch on to see that there was a huge snake curled over it—a python by the look of it.

A scream gurgled in her throat as she leapt away, tripped, dropped the torch and fell against something that also moved, but much more vigorously.

In fact it was Raefe, who picked her up in his arms and strode away with her.

'Oh, thank heavens,' she whispered as he put her on her feet on the veranda, although he kept an arm around her while he switched on the light. 'I got the most awful fright!'

'You're a bloody idiot,' he said grimly. 'Don't you know snakes are liable to be about at night? And especially after that rain?'

'No! I hadn't even th-thought about it,' she stammered. 'Crocodiles, mosquitoes, things that crawl through my hair—yes, but how was I to know...? Anyway—' she changed tack '—I thought snakes were more frightened of you and always took evasive action!'

'And how long were you sitting there lost in thought, as still as a mouse and with no light on?' he shot back.

Francesca swallowed. 'I don't know. Quite a long time, I suppose. But you were out and about too,' she objected.

'I know what I'm liable to encounter; you obviously don't.'

Francesca stared up into his eyes then went to move away, but she looked at the hand she'd touched the snake with and her knees buckled unexpectedly as her skin crawled and nausea rose in her throat.

He swore beneath his breath and picked her up to sit down with her on a cane settee. 'It's all right,' he said, still exasperatedly, but the anger was gone. 'Why don't you think of Indiana Jones? He loathed the feel of them too.'

Francesca hiccuped, but the nausea subsided slowly and then she chuckled. 'So he did. I don't know why but it does make me feel better. Mind you, I may not be game to leave the house for a while with the thought of it lurking out there.'

'It won't be for much longer.'

'Why? I mean, how come?'

'Because, Chessie—' he looked down at her with a lurking smile in his eyes '—as soon as you are sufficiently recovered, I'm going to deal with it.'

'How?'

He paused. 'If you're squeamish, don't ask. If it was daylight I'd shoot it, but I don't want to frighten the life out of Jess.'

'All right, I won't ask.' She shivered. 'But how will you find it?'

'I'll take a torch and follow its track. Simple.'

Francesca grimaced. 'Rather you than me.' And she sat still, on his lap, leaning back against his arm, as she pictured him trailing the snake, armed with a spade or a machete, through the dripping bushes and casuarinas, and she shivered again then took a deep breath. 'Will you...?'

But she looked up at him and stopped abruptly. Because he was looking at her legs sprawled across the settee and she suddenly realised that her skirt had got hitched up along one thigh, so that the lace edge of her satin panties was exposed. Then his gaze travelled upwards, and she saw that one strap of her top had slipped down, exposing the paler flesh of the swell of her breast. But what made matters worse was the way she was suddenly filled with the desire to have him slip both straps down and explore her breasts with his long, strong fingers.

She took a shaky breath—and their gazes locked.

Until he said, 'No, Chessie, I will not.'

'I didn't mean that,' she said unevenly, and tried to get up. He refused to let her.

'What did you mean?'

She swallowed. 'I was going to say will you be all right, as in *safe*, or do you need someone to hold the torch for you? *That's* all I meant!'

He raised a sceptical eyebrow and unexpectedly pushed some wayward hair behind her ear. 'A moment ago you were sick and shivering with fright.'

'I also believe in confronting my fears, not hiding behind them. So while it's not exactly what I'd choose to be doing—hunting a large python at this time of night—it might be better for me *to* do it.'

'Are you serious?'

'Of course I am,' she said crossly. 'I may be a lot of things—in your estimation I'm obviously a lot of very *bad* things—but I am not a coward.' This time she managed to evade his hands, and she stood up, smoothed her skirt, adjusted her straps and confronted him angrily with her hands on her hips.

'What now?' he murmured.

'You're unbelievable sometimes, that's what now,' she returned scathingly. 'I wasn't devouring *your* legs with my eyes—I wasn't even aware of what had happened to my skirt or my strap. But *I'm* the one who always ends up the villain of the piece, if not to say worse! I'm the one who is—'

'The temptress? The seductress? Or—' he smiled lazily '—perhaps those words have left our vocabulary now, because they're sexist. All the same—'

But it was Francesca's turn to break in. 'You can go and find that jolly snake on your own, Raefe Stevensen. I'm going to bed.'

It was a sparkling day that confronted Francesca the next morning, but she found herself in no mood to appreciate it. In fact she couldn't imagine how she was going to get through the day, but then Annette and Barbara turned up—she'd forgotten it was one of Barbara's cleaning days—and she gave silent thanks for their company.

It was Raefe who proposed they test out the new barbecue with an early evening meal and that the Brown family join them— Why not make a bit of a party of it? he suggested, with a wry little smile. This time Francesca could barely suppress a shout of thanks—she had had no idea how she was going to cope with an evening alone with Raefe.

So, with Barbara and Annette's help, she made salads, she prepared kebabs and marinated them. She wrapped fillets of fresh sweetlip in foil. She set out a tray of sausages, chops and steaks, and as a final effort produced a light-as-air pavlova which she filled with fresh cream, slices of banana and passion fruit.

'Let's dress up a bit,' Annette said pertly as she helped her mother wash up.

'That means we've got to go home,' Barbara responded, and looked at her watch. 'It's four-thirty already. Raefe said five-thirty.'

'That gives us a whole hour, Mum. Pretty please! What do you reckon, Chessie?' Fran was becoming a name of the past, Francesca noticed.

'Uh—how dressy? It *is* only a barbecue,' she said cautiously.

'Let's pretend we're in Hawaii, or something exciting like that, and wear our prettiest frocks—and I tell you what, I'll fix some flowers in our hair.'

'Me too?' Jess enquired excitedly.

'Of course you too, pet,' Annette said affectionately.

'So long as you don't turn me into an elderly hippie,' Barbara said ruefully.

'Oh, Mum, you're not old! Can we? I'll ask Raefe to give us an extra half-hour. The later we eat, the cooler it will be anyway.'

'Oh, all right,' Barbara conceded. 'It is pretty boring for you up here. OK with you, Chessie?'

'Fine,' Francesca relented with a grin.

'Look—I'm just green with envy,' Annette said as she expertly wove some coral hibiscus blooms into Francesca's hair.

'Why?'

'Your dress.' Annette herself wore a long, pretty floral dress with a heart-shaped neckline and buttons down the front.

Francesca looked down ruefully at the pale blue dress she'd worn a few nights ago. 'I only brought this one dress—oh, and a couple of skirts and tops. All the rest are shorts and trousers.'

'It's gorgeous,' Annette said through a mouthful of hairpins. 'Where did you buy it? I never see clothes like that in Cairns.'

'Paris.' Francesca grimaced.

Annette's hands stilled, and her eyes in the mirror were wide. 'Paris, France?'

'I'm afraid so.'

'No wonder! On a working holiday over there too, I suppose?'

'Something like that,' Francesca agreed with a niggle of guilt. 'That looks great. Thanks, Annette—and it feels so cool!'

Annette stepped back and studied her handiwork. She'd swept Francesca's hair back into a plait and had tucked the blossoms in high on the crown. 'Can…can I put a bit of make-up on you?'

'Oh, I don't—'

'Please,' Annette begged. 'My ambition is to be a beautician as well as a hairdresser, and we've still got ten minutes. You've got the most gorgeous cosmetics!'

Francesca glanced at the black and gold containers on the dressing table, then into Annette's glowing eyes. 'All right,' she laughed. 'But very discreetly, please.'

Ten minutes later she had to acknowledge that this girl, who'd grown up in the bush and could probably rope calves, had magic in her fingers. She'd applied foundation, blusher, eyeshadow and so on with the lightest touch so that the whole was barely discernible but artistically enhancing—Francesca's eyes appeared larger and an even deeper blue, and the greatest effect was given to her already good bone structure.

'Annette,' she said when the work was finished, 'I've got the feeling you're going to be wasted on Cairns one day, you know.'

'Thanks.' Annette's smile was huge. 'I don't intend to spend the rest of my life in Cairns anyway, but it's so much easier with a face like yours—I don't know why you're a governess. You could be a model, a film star—anything!'

Francesca stood up and turned the conversation with the first thought that came to mind. 'How would Jericho feel about that?'

Annette sobered. 'Leaving Cairns? I don't know. He's not talking to me at the moment.'

'Because you wouldn't go on holiday with him?'

'Because I wouldn't believe him when he said it could be separate rooms all the way if that's what I wanted. Well, why should I?' Annette said, with a curious mixture of belligerence and mournfulness. 'He's as big as an ox. And how did he imagine I'd tell Mum and Dad what I was doing? Men are the limit, really!'

Francesca reached for her hand. They were the same height and in the mirror looked like sisters in their pretty dresses and with flowers in their hair. 'If he really is serious about you, he'll come back. Now, shall we go to this party?'

The new barbecue proved itself admirably, and the fast-setting sun provided the perfect backdrop, turning the placid water to a living pink. Raefe brought out some wine and beer—cola for Jess—and they toasted the beach shelter, with its palm thatch roof and open sides, as well as the barbecue.

Bob told some funny stories about his days as a ringer when all the mustering had been done on horseback, all the food went down well and Jess, pretty in a yellow dress and with little white flowers in her hair, enjoyed herself immensely.

'I'm afraid all good things come to an end, though,' Raefe said when the pavlova had been consumed.

'Too true,' Bob Brown agreed. 'It's half past eight and I've got a bore to check tomorrow. Going to give your old man a hand, Annie?' he said affectionately to his daughter. 'We'll ride out; it's pretty inaccessible otherwise.'

'Love to, Dad,' Annette replied. 'Although I suppose that means I'll have to get up before the crack of dawn!'

They all laughed and Jess quite naturally curled up in Francesca's lap, making no attempt to smother a huge yawn. 'Bedtime, honeybunch,' she said softly, then saw Raefe's eyes on her in the firelight. 'Unless…?'

But he shook his head and looked away. So Francesca gathered up Jess, who was all but asleep, Annette, Bob and Barbara gathered up most of the dishes and they walked up to the house, saying goodnight to Raefe and, in Annette's case, adding exuberant thanks.

'There's still a few things out there,' Barbara said anxiously, 'plus these dishes. I'll just—'

'Don't worry about it,' Francesca said softly. '*I* don't have to get up before the crack of dawn tomorrow. Thanks for all your help!'

The Browns departed in one of the station vehicles, and Francesca changed Jess into her pyjamas and put the little girl to bed. She fell asleep again as soon as her head touched the pillow.

It occurred to Francesca, as she hesitated on the veranda in the act of going down to the beach to collect the rest of the stuff, that she might have been better off accepting Barbara's offer. Because she could see Raefe's outline clearly in the firelight—he'd lifted the grid off the barbecue and added more wood to it and was sitting motionless, watching the flames.

Then she shook herself mentally and decided she couldn't avoid him completely—and *she* wasn't the one in the wrong anyway...

She had the wind rather taken out of her sails when he turned at her approach, stood up and offered her a glass of wine.

'Pity to waste it,' he murmured, lifting the three-quarters-empty bottle from the wine-cooler. 'Why don't you sit down? I guarantee there are no pythons in the immediate vicinity, and it is a beautiful night.'

'Well—er—thanks,' she said, and was annoyed to hear how uncertain she sounded. So she sat down on a wooden bench and said, 'I've been wanting to talk to you anyway.'

He cast her an amused little look. 'Fire away.'

That had the instant effect of rendering her mind blank—no, that wasn't quite it, she mused darkly. She certainly had a lot of things she would like to say to him, but to plunge in unprepared would be foolhardy to say the least. She took a sip of the chilled white wine instead.

'Changed your mind?' he said lightly after a couple of minutes of silence. 'Oh, well, perhaps we should concentrate on the moon and the stars—'

'No, I haven't changed my mind,' she interrupted coolly. 'I was merely...wondering whether to waste my time and breath.' Not entirely true, but perhaps a better way to go, she thought bitterly.

'Chessie, I can see that you are labouring under the serious burden—rightly or wrongly—of feeling ill-used and hard done by—why don't you just spit it out?'

'How old are you?' she said, changing tack abruptly.

He raised an eyebrow. 'What's that got to do with the price of eggs?'

'I thought it might explain why, when you aren't kissing me against my will, ogling my legs, et cetera, et cetera,' she said with deep irony, 'you treat me like a foolish teenager—"Spit it out"!' she marvelled. 'Who the hell do you think you are?'

He grinned. 'That's my Francesca Valentine... Er...so what do you suspect? That I'm in my dotage? I'm thirty-four,' he added before she could take further umbrage. 'Which is about twelve years older than you are—although the gap may be closer in…actual experience,' he said softly.

'Eleven,' Francesca snapped. 'I'm twenty-three. As for your other—'

'Then you look younger than your age sometimes, Chessie,' he mused, 'which is supposed to be the aim of most women—although not tonight.'

'I—what do you mean?'

'I mean that when you came out in all your glory this evening, with your hair exquisitely groomed and all expertly made up, you looked every inch a very sophisticated twenty-three-year-old. I'm only surprised you didn't touch up your make-up when you put Jess to bed—it was all for my benefit, I gather? You surely haven't got Bob in your sights as well?'

The absolute breathtaking *unfairness* of this attack did just that—took Francesca's breath away. Then she choked on sheer rage, and was further infuriated when he recommended she have a sip of wine. Which she did—several in fact—at the same time as she was aware of a curious refrain growing in her mind. Oh, no, it was saying. Oh, no, you don't, Raefe Stevensen. You don't get away with this.

'You noticed,' she murmured, looking at him over the rim of her glass.

'I noticed,' he agreed.

She shrugged gently. 'I thought it was all—rather discreet.'

'It was.'

'But still you noticed. You must have been studying me pretty closely, Raefe. I mean, to be aware of the difference.'

There was a short silence. Then he said drily, 'And that pleases you, I gather?'

She drew the blue dress up to her knees and crossed her legs elegantly sideways, pointing her toes and, apparently absent-mindedly, raising her arm so that the lie of the blue material was altered across her breasts. She patted the hibiscus blooms in her hair.

'Well, it's nice to know it wasn't all *wasted*. You know, Raefe—do you mind if I call you that again? I will anyway—you said something about women-starved bush cowboys yesterday. Has it entered your mind that it could well apply to you? I mean, I know you've conceded you're not a block of wood, but when you can pick out a really expertly done make-up job on a girl in fading daylight perhaps there's a bit more to it?'

The air stirred between them, but it was only the breeze, not the sheer friction of static electricity as they gazed at each other, and she saw again that tiger-like response in all his muscles she'd seen the first morning they'd met on this very beach.

But she was very angry—angrier than she could ever remember—and she threw all caution to the wind as she got up gracefully, stretched, then moved to his side to put her hands about his face, to lean towards him and place her lips lightly on his.

'You know, my friend,' she said a bare moment later, very quietly and calmly, which was far from how she was feeling, still cupping his face and staring deep into his eyes, 'think what you like about me but there's one thing *I* despise—a man who wants me against his better judgement. A man who blames all his turmoil on me.' She straightened and walked away without a backward glance.

It was a while before Raefe Stevensen moved. It would also be a while, he acknowledged, before the mental image of that lovely figure curved over him in its flowing blue dress would leave him. Before the perfume of her skin, the feel of her fingers and the cool taste of her lips would leave him. And it would be the action of a fool to ignore the point she'd made.

So, one up to you, Chessie Valentine, he thought. That was cleverer than I expected. And in the mean-time—his lips twisted involuntarily—it might be a good idea to go for a swim...

CHAPTER FIVE

FRANCESCA woke the next morning with a sense of impending doom that she immediately recognised—it was always the same when she'd done something she shouldn't have. It took just a moment or two to remember what she had actually done the previous day. Then it hit her, and she sat up with a groan and rubbed her face exasperatedly.

Why hadn't she told Raefe Stevensen the simple truth about the make-up and hairstyle? Why on *earth* had she allowed him to get to her to the extent of provoking her into a deliberate vamp act?

She cast aside the sheet and sprang up restlessly. It was very early but had every appearance of being another sparkling day. She stood at the window in her French blue satin and lace camisole night-top and matching sleep-shorts. Her hair still held a trace of kinkiness from being plaited and she moved impatiently to the dressing table, where she twisted it into a knot on the top of her head and secured it with a large grip.

She was impatient, she realised, for two reasons—and neither of them to do with her hair. Firstly she would have liked nothing better than to go down for an early-morning swim, but was afraid of running into Raefe. And secondly she was impatient with herself for getting herself embroiled the way she had.

She took a deep breath and stared at her reflection in the mirror—how far wrong had she been in her final summing up of last night's situation? The way she'd gone about it might have been a bit dangerous, but hadn't she spoken her final words from the heart?

She turned away from the mirror angrily, because she had no doubt Raefe Stevensen wouldn't believe them. And so, instead of staying inside like a good little governess and cook—Who *does* he think he is? I'm *no one's* hired help!—she stripped, pulled her yellow costume on and strode proudly down to the beach.

'Have a nice swim, Chessie?' Jess said at breakfast.

'Yes, thank you,' Francesca replied as she dished up bacon and eggs. 'I didn't know you were awake, otherwise I'd have taken you with me.'

'I was in bed with Daddy—he got up really early to make himself a cup of tea and I heard him. So we went back to bed together and read *Bedknobs and Broomsticks*. He was going to take me for a swim, but when we saw you go down he said we should leave you in peace—didn't you?' She turned to her father.

Francesca glanced at him over Jess's head with a tinge of irony, to encounter an unperturbed grey gaze.

'Sprung—so I did,' Raefe conceded.

'What does sprung mean?' Jess enquired.

'Caught out, in this sense, Jess,' Raefe said gravely, 'although it has other meanings. You can say, for example, a car is really well sprung—that means it's got good springs so you don't bump up and down—or you can say spring has sprung, meaning that spring has arrived and flowers are springing up. Or you can say—' he looked up at Francesca, a fleeting, mocking little look '—the truth has sprung up—at last. Would you like me to cut your bacon, Jess?'

I knew it, Francesca thought a little wildly, and dished up her own breakfast. 'You can also say,' she murmured, sitting down,'"Truth is within ourselves"—Browning. Then there's another one: "Truth, crushed to earth, shall rise again"—William Cullen Bryant. If you substitute "spring up" for "rise", we're not so far off the point, are we? In more ways than one. Jess, will you have marmalade or honey on your toast?'

What might have transpired then was never to be known, because Annette dashed into the kitchen with the news that Bob had been injured in a fall from his horse.

'How is he?' Francesca asked anxiously when Raefe arrived home after dark. Jess was asleep after an early meal, and there was a leg of roast pork with done-to-perfection crisp crackling in the oven.

Raefe sloughed off his peaked cap and ran his fingers through his damp hair—his khaki bush shirt and trousers were also sweat-stained. He'd called for a helicopter and flown Bob to the Cairns Base Hospital himself. About twenty minutes earlier Francesca had heard the helicopter land at the cattle yards. There was adequate lighting for a night landing beside the huge machinery shed.

'He's fractured his shoulder and broken his leg. He'll be in plaster for three months, but it will all heal eventually. I left Annette with him and brought Barbara back to put some things together. I'll take her back tomorrow and she'll stay with Annette in Cairns while he's recuperating.'

'That'll make things hard here—how will you cope?' Francesca said slowly.

'Not without some difficulty,' he said drily, then sniffed appreciatively as she produced the pork and vegetables. 'I've left Banyo Air a bit short-handed lately, and now Bramble will be short-handed—although it could be worse. At least it's the wet.'

He washed his hands at the kitchen sink and walked over to the informal dining alcove where she'd laid out dinner. The table was beside an open screened window and above it there were two wrought-iron wall sconces with candle globes that directed soft light onto the table and laid shadows of their shapes on the rough-plastered white wall.

Francesca had laid the table with an avocado-green cloth and the day-to-day crockery, with its bold yellow and green flowers on a white background. Raefe picked up the carving knife and sharpened it briefly on the steel.

'You will also be short-handed,' he added, laying the steel down, and there was a peculiar sort of emphasis underlying his words.

Francesca brought the apple sauce and the gravy to the table, hesitated, then smoothed the white shorts that she wore with a coral halter-top. She started to say something then thought better of it. She sat down, watched him start to carve, and only then said quietly, 'Would you like to explain?'

He looked across at her interrogatively. 'Isn't it obvious?' He handed her her plate.

'Not entirely.' She served herself a roast potato, a piece of pumpkin and some cauliflower with white sauce. 'I get the feeling there was more to what you *weren't* saying than to what you were.'

He sat down and she saw the flash of cynicism in his grey gaze as it rested briefly on her, on her hair tied up in a knot on her head and the smooth golden skin of her shoulders, before he turned his attention to the vegetables.

She took an angry breath, but forced herself to say evenly, 'No—I'm not about to make you grovel, if that's what you're expecting. I can cope quite well without Barbara for a while, unless you have another idea or a better one. It's up to you.'

He swore beneath his breath, poured gravy onto his meat and said grimly, 'All right. Before this happened I was about to suggest that we come to a parting of the ways sooner rather than later. I'd worked out that since Annette was here she might be able to look after Jess until Sarah got back, or until I could make other arrangements. That's out of the question now, and I spoke to Sarah by phone while I was in Cairns, and she—well, she would like to stay on in Brisbane for a while.'

Francesca toyed with her food, then said thoughtfully, 'It's funny you should say that. I'd also decided that, from Jess's point of view, it would be better to come to a parting of the ways sooner rather than later. I don't suppose you'll believe me, but—'

'Look,' he said roughly, 'let's not beat about the bush. Jess is not the only consideration, although she will always be my first and foremost one. The real problem is that we can't live together, apparently, you and I, without indulging in a rather degrading type of warfare.' He paused as she moved suddenly, then said, 'For which I readily take part of the blame, Francesca, but all the same the *sooner* it's nipped in the bud the better.'

It was the first time he'd called her that, and for some reason she discovered that she preferred to be Chessie, even with all the nuances he'd used when addressing her. But she was not a Valentine for nothing.

'So be it,' she murmured. 'I'll leave tomorrow morning. Is it at all possible to send Jess down to Sarah? I could take her, if you like, if you trust me that far— Never mind; forget I suggested it.'

'Chessie…' he said through his teeth, but she got up and walked away from the table to the back door.

'Chessie, come back and finish your dinner,' he said after a moment, and then, when she didn't stir, added quietly, 'Don't make me have to come and get you.'

She turned, and her eyes flashed blue fire.

They stared at each other until she said, 'Don't patronise me, Raefe. I don't know—and I no longer care—what your problems are, but I've done my level best with your daughter.'

He closed his eyes briefly. 'Look, I acknowledge that and I'm grateful for it. Please, sit down.'

She hesitated, then resumed her seat and started to eat.

'In fact, as a governess, you couldn't have been better.'

She glanced at him wryly.

'But you're not a governess, Chessie.' He got up abruptly, went to the fridge and opened a bottle of wine. He poured two glasses and put one beside her plate without consulting her. 'And therein lies the kernel. It's a farce, this; it always has been—and, whilst I know I've done my share, there's one thing I keep coming back to. Why *would* Frank Valentine's daughter do something like this?'

'I may be my father's daughter,' Francesca said after an age, and sipped some wine, 'but I'm my own person too. He was not the sole force in my creation. I had a mother once—'

'I'm—'

'No,' she went on as he broke in, 'let's leave all that alone. I think we've done it to death anyway. But if you do genuinely believe I've looked after Jess well, then at least credit me with possessing some *genuine* concern for her—is it out of the question to send her down to Sarah? Even if her wrist hasn't healed it must be easier to get help in Brisbane than it is up here.'

Raefe finished eating and put his knife and fork together. He picked up his glass and studied the wine in it. 'Sarah,' he said at last, 'is trying to get her marriage together again. The last thing she needs—although she'd probably never forgive me for not asking her— is to be landed with Jess at the moment.'

'I thought—' Francesca stopped.

He raised an eyebrow at her.

'I thought she was sad,' she said. 'Which seemed a pity because she's such a nice person.'

'She is.' Raefe drank some wine. 'He is too.'

Francesca's natural curiosity fought a battle with her

other emotions, which included what she believed to be a genuine desire to have nothing more to do with or say to Raefe Stevensen, but her curiosity won. 'So what's the problem?'

'He had an affair.'

'I thought you said he was nice?'

'What they fell out over was Sarah's inability to have children. He claimed it didn't matter; she was consumed by guilt. For some reason it started to turn things sour between them and when he…did what he did, and then came back to her because he bitterly regretted it, she couldn't forgive him. Despite the fact that she's miserable without him.'

Francesca blinked. 'It might have been asking a lot of her. What if it had happened the other way around?'

Raefe moved his shoulders. 'Who knows? The only thing I tried to clarify for her was that Mark is only waiting for her to make some sort of a move, and that she might spend the rest of her life regretting it if she doesn't.'

Francesca digested this but looked unconvinced.

'He's been waiting for nearly two years,' Raefe said. 'Sarah's been using Jess as an excuse to stay up here for at least half that time.'

Francesca's brows rose. 'I see,' she said slowly.

Raefe smiled unexpectedly, and commented equally unexpectedly, 'The ways of men and women are strange, aren't they?'

'Yes,' Francesca agreed with unconscious fervour, causing him to look wry. 'So, well, what will you do?'

He studied her comprehensively. 'What I was about to do before I got—unnecessarily brutal, perhaps.'

'Ask me to stay on for a while?' Francesca suggested after a brief pause.

'Yes.'

Several expressions chased through her eyes, then her gaze steadied and she smiled briefly. 'I hope that's as galling to your pride as it is to mine not to respond with incredulous disdain. I—'

'You mean, not to say, How dare you? Who do you think you are? Et cetera?'

'Something like that, but perhaps I ought to make it plain that I couldn't square my conscience to simply walking away from Jess. I'll stay on one condition.'

He grimaced. 'I can imagine—although we've made those protestations before.'

'Protestations of innocence regarding any ulterior motive we may have towards each other? So we have.' She smiled coolly this time. 'No, I wasn't about to launch into that again. My condition is this—that you let me help you find someone to take over.'

Surprise flared briefly in his eyes, affording Francesca a spurt of satisfaction. He said slowly, 'How?'

'Well, Cairns is a fairly limited reservoir to be tapping for staff. I could go further afield—'

'I could go further afield too,' he objected. 'But at least someone from Cairns would be used to the tropical climate, wouldn't feel as if they'd been dumped at the end of the earth and could get home reasonably easily for breaks now and then.'

'All of which is why Joyce Cotton was at her wits' end!' Francesca shot back.

He shrugged. 'And where would you go?'

'I'd go to my old headmistress, for a start.'

'The one who made sure Frank Valentine's daughter wouldn't have to go on the dole if ever the Valentine empire failed?'

Francesca showed her teeth. 'The same.'

'I would have thought she might have alienated herself from you somewhat,' he drawled.

'She did no such thing—well…' Francesca paused and smiled reminiscently. 'We had a few right royal battles, yes, but no more than I would have had—than *any* teenager might have had—with a mother,' she amended.

Raefe's eyes narrowed. 'So, you had to make do with a headmistress for a mother-figure, Chessie?'

Francesca remembered the number of occasions she'd returned to boarding-school either in a rage or a daze of misery at the inadequacies of her home life. 'Not a mother-figure, no, but at least…a constant figure. And now that I've left school we get along really well.'

Raefe sat forward after a silent moment or two. 'How close to your father are you?'

'Why do you want to know?' she asked proudly.

'There've been rumours for years of a—a succession of mistresses.'

'If you're trying to say—if you're somehow or other trying to implicate me in that kind of lifestyle—you're worse than I thought,' she said, and just for a moment it occurred to Raefe that the glitter in those beautiful blue eyes might be tears. Then it was gone as she blinked, although a pale shadow of anger lingered about her mouth.

'No—I was wondering how hard that might have

been to live with on top of not having a mother,' he said quietly.

'You asked me the other day if I thought Jess lived in her make-believe world too much. I can tell you from personal experience that when you're deprived of a mother at that age it's—well, it's exactly what *I* did. But I had to give my fantasies away fairly early on. It seemed foolish to persist when there appeared to be no way the real thing—a loving family—was ever going to come my way.'

'You didn't...' He paused and pleated his napkin with his long fingers. 'You didn't mention this the day I asked about Jess.'

'No. I have no idea why Jess is without a mother, for one thing, and for another you so obviously doubted my motivation. But for the record, yes, perhaps she is a little preoccupied with her toy family, but you should be thankful she's got you—and that.'

'Chessie...so that's why you fitted into Jess's "family" so well. I wondered,' he mused, as if he was talking to himself.

'I know,' she said bleakly.

'Look, I apologise.'

She gazed at him, and the look in her eyes was both proud and shuttered. 'You don't have to feel sorry for me—I loathe that. Not that many people do, and I—'

'Go out of your way to avoid it,' he said drily. 'I think I'm beginning to understand you a bit better, Chessie Valentine.' He stopped, and before he got the chance to go on she spoke.

'I wouldn't bank on understanding me too well,

Raefe.' Her blue gaze was tinged with scorn now, causing him to raise a rueful eyebrow.

'All right, I won't,' he conceded mildly. 'So, you think your headmistress—a lady I've never met, who lives nearly the length of the continent away—might be able to help me out of this contretemps?'

'Yes,' Francesca said shortly. 'And if I were you I'd reserve that tone of kindly indulgence until after I've told you a bit more.'

'Kindly indulgence?'

'*Yes.* Barely cloaking a weary sort of superiority,' she said accusingly.

'Dear me,' he murmured, and there was genuine amusement in his eyes. 'I'll have to watch myself.'

She glanced at him exasperatedly and went to stand up. 'I'm wasting my time.'

'No.' He leant across the table and detained her with a hand on her wrist. 'I'm sorry. Go ahead; I promise to behave myself.'

'Well…' Francesca subsided, and fortified herself with a sip of wine. 'There are two kinds of people she has access to. Teachers who would give their eye-teeth to have a bit of a break from school routines, and girls of school-leaving age who would also like to do something different for a while—Jess wouldn't come to any harm with more of a nanny at the moment. Although…' She stopped and looked thoughtful.

'Go on.'

'You might be better off with a middle-aged teacher.'

'Oh? Why?' He drained his glass.

'Because we wouldn't want some sweet young

thing falling in love with you, now, would we?' Francesca raised her glass in an ironic salute and drained her own wine. Then she blinked. 'On the other hand, perhaps that's just what you need! It would keep you safe from predatory females such as myself, and solve the problem you obviously have with living like a monk.'

His mouth hardened. 'I thought this might be too good to be true.'

'Well, you were right—oh, hell,' she said abruptly, and stood up to gather plates.

'What now?'

'Sorry, that was a bitchy thing to say.' She paused with their plates held in her hands and looked him over unemotionally.

At least, that was how it started out, but, even at the end of a difficult day, in his stained khakis, with his hair still damp and darkened and lines of weariness beside his mouth, Raefe Stevensen was dangerously attractive. But more—he did some strange things to her heartstrings.

Not that it's going to do me any good, thinking along those lines, she reflected, and flicked her gaze away. 'There are times when you don't pull any punches, though,' she said, barely audibly, and walked to the sink.

He was silent for as long as it took her to clear the table. Then he refilled their glasses. 'Sit down a moment longer, Chessie—no, I don't want coffee, thank you,' he said as she put her hand on the percolator.

She hesitated, then did as she was bid, looking at him enquiringly over the rim of her glass.

'I appreciate your suggestion, and in other circumstances I'd give it a go, but right now it still leaves me short-handed. In the house and on the property. So I thought the answer might be to look for a married couple.'

'That's not a bad idea,' she said slowly. 'You mean to live here in the house?'

'Temporarily at least. That would free them from the responsibility of their own home, which was Barbara's problem, and it would mean there'd always be someone for Jess—someone to do the cooking and so on.'

'Is that a tall order? Finding a couple like that?'

'It may be easier than a single person, but it may also take a few weeks. Does your father know where you are, Chessie?'

She blinked and followed his change of direction with difficulty. 'Why?'

'I just wondered.'

'Yes, he does—roughly.'

'What does that mean?'

'Well, he knows I'm in this part of the world, and I did mention the name of Bramble Downs—not to him but to his secretary, in case of emergency. But I didn't tell her this was actually where I was...' She grimaced.

'You mean you didn't exactly explain what you were doing?'

'No.' She looked down at her glass, as if suddenly remembering it, and drank some wine, trying to appear nonchalant.

'What *did* you say you were doing?'

'Touring, getting to know this part of the world—that kind of thing.' Francesca shrugged.

'Alone?'

'Look—' Francesca stared at him levelly '—my father knows better than to…to try to pin me down these days. I'm quite capable of looking after myself.'

'All the same, I'd be surprised if he didn't exercise some sort of surveillance.'

'Just in case I get myself kidnapped and he has to fork out a large ransom?' Francesca said with irony.

'You said it. Or get yourself married for your money.'

'I told you, I'm an old hand at detecting gold-diggers. And it's not exactly a problem I have here,' she said wearily. 'But if it sets your mind at rest I've rung in a couple of times to let them know I'm safe and sound. I'm going to do the dishes now, and go to bed.'

'All right, I'll give you a hand. I take it you approve of my plan?'

'For a married couple—heartily,' Francesca said with a great deal of feeling, causing a strange little smile to twist his lips.

The next few days were strangely peaceful.

Well, not so strange, Francesca mused. Raefe was hardly home at all, except to grab the odd meal and sleep, and she and Jess did what they usually did; a mixture of play, swimming and some schoolwork. They also—and this excited Jess—began to prepare for the new School of the Air school year, to be conducted over the homestead radio.

They also drove down twice daily to the Browns'

house, where they fed the variety of pets the Browns owned—a tame galah, two cattle dogs, three cats and six goldfish in a tank—and watered Barbara's garden and pot plants. It was the first time Francesca had driven her new four-wheel drive around the property at all, but, mindful of Raefe's jibe about the opposition, she didn't attempt to go further afield.

Then it was the weekend, and on the Saturday Raefe flew home at midday. Jess, at least, was delighted to hear that he would be with them until Monday morning. He had plans for the afternoon which involved taking Jess for a helicopter ride, and something else.

'It's a treat—tomorrow,' he said with a lurking grin.

Jess held his hand with both of her own, and her fair curls bobbed with excitement as she begged to be told what it was.

'Well, it's a sort of surprise—but why don't you ask Chessie if she could make us a picnic lunch for tomorrow?'

Jess was further enchanted, and not fooled either. 'You're going to take us to Paradise Island—I know it, Daddy, I know!'

'Paradise Island?' Francesca enquired that evening. She was lying back on a lounger on the veranda with a long, cool lime drink beside her. Raefe had insisted she have the afternoon off, and he and Jess had flown to a neighbouring property to spend the afternoon and have dinner. They'd returned not long ago and Jess had fallen asleep as soon as her head touched the pillow. 'Does one need wings to get there?'

Raefe sat down opposite her—on the same cane settee where she'd sat on his lap to recover from her encounter with the python, as it happened. He was barefoot—it was very hot—and wearing shorts and a T-shirt, and he sprawled his long legs out and clasped his hands behind his head. 'In a manner of speaking—rotors, anyway.'

'I see. So it's somewhere out there?' She gestured seawards.

He nodded.

'Your own private island?'

'No. Although very few people go there. It's just a hop, skip and a jump, actually, in the chopper, but I thought we'd have a look at the reef from the air at the same time.'

'Sounds nice,' Francesca murmured.

'Did you enjoy your time off?'

'I…' She hesitated and lowered her lashes suddenly, because the truth was she'd felt lonely and abandoned. 'It was very peaceful. And I caught up with the ironing.'

'That wasn't the purpose of it,' he said irritably.

Francesca grimaced. 'I didn't mean to sound martyred.' She sat up cross-legged and lifted her hair off her neck. She'd been for a swim in the last of the daylight, and had only added a light, sleeveless voile top to her costume. 'Does this heat build up to a good, solid thunderstorm that cools things down?'

He looked across at her. 'Rain, yes—not that it cools things down much. This is the norm for this time of the year. A good, solid cyclone is always on the cards, however.'

She looked interested. 'I've never experienced one of those.'

'I would cross your fingers that you don't,' he replied humorously.

'Have you lived through some?'

'Of course. It comes with the territory.'

'Were you terrified?'

He thought for a moment, then shrugged. 'Not exactly terrified, but it's not something you enjoy. Nor is the sound of the wind something you ever forget. Then there are tidal surges, although the combination of circumstances that causes them is rare—I haven't lived through one of those,' he said, regarding her wide eyes with some amusement.

'You're very close to the sea here.'

'And we always retreat inland if there's the slightest danger. The most famous cyclone in this part of the world was Mahina. It hit a bit further north, in the Cape Melville-Bathurst Bay area, in 1899, catching a pearling fleet at anchor. Over three hundred people drowned and dolphins were reputedly stranded in the small cliffs of some of the islands in the area—such was the height of the sea at the cyclone's centre.'

'Now you tell me!' Francesca said after a breathless moment, then dissolved into helpless laughter.

'Well, I'm pleased you're not a nervous wreck—but what's so funny?'

She wiped her streaming eyes. 'And you're worried about my father being afraid I'll be kidnapped—I don't know why, but it does strike me as funny.'

He laughed too after a moment, then said curiously, 'But it obviously doesn't strike instant terror into your heart? Or even faint fear?'

Francesca chuckled and sniffed. 'Did you think—

perhaps hope—I might pack my bags and drive away at speed? Sorry, strike that,' she murmured, and sobered. 'Er—terror? No. I imagine—I'm *sure*—satellite weather predictions didn't exist in 1899. I'm also sure you wouldn't expose Jess to danger—I mean, you've obviously got contingency plans?'

'We do. And wherever I am at this time of the year I keep a sharp ear open for low-pressure systems in the Coral Sea. Sometimes they develop into cyclones with astonishing speed, in spite of satellites and so on.'

'I'm glad to hear it.' She uncrossed her legs and sank back, feeling curiously relaxed. 'Tell me about your neighbours.'

'They're a fairly elderly couple and they're retiring to Cairns. I've offered to buy the property.'

Francesca raised an eyebrow. 'It's quite a little empire you're building, Mr Stevensen.'

'"Little" being the operative word?'

'Do you know...' she sat up again, abruptly this time '...if you're *happy* that's the operative word?'

'As your father isn't?' he said after a moment.

Francesca subsided and looked away.

'You're very loyal—most of the time,' Raefe commented, then stood up, stretched and yawned. 'I think I'll go to bed. By the way, if I sounded unappreciative of the ironing, I'm not. Thanks, Chessie.' And he walked inside.

Francesca lay on her lounger and felt shocked by several things. She was shocked by her sharp sense of loss, because she wasn't tired and would have loved him to stay and talk to her, relaxed as they had been. And she was shocked by her growing need to know what had happened to Jess's mother and her urge to ask him a simple question: *was* he happy?

CHAPTER SIX

HELICOPTERS were no novelty to Francesca, but sitting beside Raefe as he flew one was. He looked so completely at home and he inspired enormous confidence. She and Jess were tucked in side by side, and both wore headphones to minimise the noise and so they could hear what Raefe was saying.

He gave Francesca a guided tour of some of the huge reefs in the area, which lightened the water to turquoise as they rose roughly circular and oval from the depths, then coloured it mottled pink and brown before they finally broke through with splashes of golden sand.

It was, on that clear, still Sunday, a wonderland. And so was Paradise Island—not its real name, but a name bestowed on it by the Stevensen family.

They hovered, then settled on a white beach enclosed by its own reef and spent a couple of hours snorkelling amongst the coral—Jess had her own small flippers and mask; Francesca used a set belonging to Sarah.

Then they found a shady patch of beach and broke out the picnic lunch.

'It is like paradise,' Francesca murmured, with a cold chicken drumstick in her hand.

Raefe finished his lunch and stretched out on a blanket on the sand, propped on his elbow. 'Uh-huh. I particularly like your potato salad, Chessie.'

'Chessie's going to give me cooking lessons—aren't you, Chessie?' Jess said importantly.

Francesca glanced a little warily at Raefe, but his eyes were on his daughter and he said easily, 'Well, you'd better ask her to teach you how to make potato salad—or is that a little advanced?' He switched his grey gaze to Francesca.

'Perhaps. I thought we'd start with biscuits.'

'And I'll be sure not to forget the chocolate chips, like Chessie did the other day,' Jess put in mischievously.

Their gazes stayed locked, Francesca's and Raefe's, and it was as if a shadow had been cast over the day for a moment, until he sat up and said mildly, 'That could have been my fault. Well, girls, I'm sorry to have to end our picnic a little prematurely, but I see some clouds on the horizon that could mean rain.'

Jess pouted, but he stood up in one fluid movement, and picked her up and tickled her until she giggled helplessly, and when he put her down she was restored to her usual good humour.

Francesca, on the other hand, on top of what had been a difficult night, turned away with her heart beating heavily. Because there was suddenly just too much to bear about Raefe Stevensen in a pair of dark green board shorts and nothing else.

It did rain, not long after they'd landed, and the rest of the afternoon was spent quietly.

They had the remains of the picnic for an early dinner, then Francesca remembered the Browns' menagerie and drove down on her own, because Jess was looking really sleepy.

For some reason she took her time about it in the rainy dusk. There was no one else around—no sign of life in the other two cottages or the shed—and she concluded that, it being a Sunday afternoon, the other hands must have decided to drive the sixty miles to the nearest pub.

She borrowed a yellow mac printed with white daisies from a peg on the wall and went around the veranda and outhouses of the head stockman's cottage, finding all Barbara's beloved pot plants—she was an avid grower of anything that grew in pots, including herbs, aloe vera, et cetera, and had them tucked away in unlikely spots to protect them from the fierce heat of the sun.

Well, they might as well all get a good drink, Francesca thought. Then she decided to put the rain streaming down from above to further good use and, when all the pets had finished eating, found an old scrubbing brush and scoured all their bowls with rain water.

By this time her hair was plastered to her head, a dark, indistinguishable colour, and she'd discarded her shoes—and she was aware of just why she was taking so much time. Anything to delay going back to the homestead and Raefe. But as the dark closed in she could find nothing else to do, and she walked up the veranda steps, closed the front door, and then, as she turned, got the fright of her life when a large, indistinct figure appeared seemingly from nowhere in front of her.

'Who…?' she tried to say, but her voice refused to work as she peered through the gloom.

'As if you don't know,' a strange voice replied, and in the next moment she was gathered into a strong pair of arms and completely enveloped by a huge man who started to kiss her urgently.

She struggled, but it was like trying to fight off a bear; all she succeeded in achieving was to make him lose his footing, but he went down with her in his arms, and they lay on the veranda, winded for a moment.

Then the stranger lifted his head to speak against her hair, his voice quivering with emotion and passion. 'Don't fight me—I won't hurt you. Why won't you believe me? I *love* you. I've loved you since the moment we first met and you laughed at me. But I'm not only after sex with you—I promise you that. Why—?'

'This is all very affecting,' a cool, cutting voice broke in—Raefe's. 'But you have half an hour to get off this property, mate. As for you…' The yellow light of a torch shone directly into Francesca's eyes, blinding her before it moved slightly. 'Well, I don't have to tell you what I think of *you*,' he said with utter contempt.

And he swung round, strode to his Land Rover, in which he must have driven up while she was unsuccessfully fighting off her would-be lover, got in and drove off with a roar in the direction of the homestead.

The unnatural silence left in his wake was broken eventually by the man, still with his arms around Francesca, although he'd manoeuvred them up to a sitting position on the top step. 'Who are you?' he said. 'And why are you wearing her raincoat?'

Francesca glanced down at the vivid yellow plastic with its brave white daisies discernible even in the dark. Then she noticed a pair of very large feet on the next step, attached to someone you might well describe as being built like an ox. And she closed her eyes as she was attacked by an insane desire to giggle hysterically.

'D-don't worry about who *I* am—*you* wouldn't go by the name of Jericho, by any chance?'

'That's me,' the big young man agreed. 'I thought you were Annette.'

'So I gathered. Would you mind letting go of me?'

'Yes, ma'am—sorry, ma'am,' he said hastily, and released her, only to add in puzzlement, 'How do you know who I am?'

Francesca explained briefly, including the fact that Annette was now in Cairns.

'I see!' Jericho let out a long whistle. 'So you know all about me—that's got to be good news, don't you reckon? I mean, she wouldn't bother to talk about me unless she liked me— Do you think she would?' he asked with disarming anxiety.

Francesca considered this as they sat side by side on the top step. 'No, I think she *does* like you, but she is only eighteen, Jerry—do you mind if I call you that?'

'No, everyone does,' he said with a grimace.

'Well, you see, amongst other things, at that age it's not easy to explain to your parents that you're going on holiday with a young man, even if you do believe he'll keep his promises. And well brought up girls are taught not to take promises like that at face value anyway.'

'But I meant it,' he protested with unmistakable fervour and youthful dignity.

'I believe you, actually,' Francesca said, and patted his large, clenched hand. 'What you should do, Jerry—if it's all right with Annette—is take this opportunity to make yourself known to her mother and father. And you should try to take things slowly.'

Jerry sat sunk in thought for a few minutes. 'I was going to do that,' he said at last. 'I was going to wait until she got back from her holiday but I just couldn't. I go back to work myself on Tuesday, so I thought... As a matter of fact, one of the reasons I drove up here was so that I *could* meet her mother and father—now I'm up here and they're back in Cairns. It'd make you spit chips, wouldn't it?'

'But you could still get back to Cairns tonight, couldn't you? Then you'd have tomorrow... Well, as I said, it's up to Annette now.'

Jerry straightened. 'Faint heart never won fair lady—isn't that what they say? My mother was full of those kind of sayings,' he added, at Francesca's look of surprise. 'The same mother who called me Jericho. OK—I'll go straight back. But not before I've squared things with that bloke—whoever he was,' he added with definite pugnacity.

'Oh, it's all right,' Francesca said soothingly. 'I'll tell him—he'll understand.'

Jerry turned to her. 'Are you *sure*? I mean, he's not your—? Well, I thought he might be...kind of involved with you, and that's why he took it so badly, if you know what I mean.'

Francesca stood up. 'I'm only the governess, Jerry. No, he's not involved with me at all, so don't you worry. Look, why don't you take Annette's raincoat back to Cairns with you? She must have forgotten it in all the rush.'

'But won't you get wet?'

'Only a little. I'm driving, not walking anyway, and it's not cold.' She took the raincoat off, giving it a vigorous shake.

Jerry stood up beside her to tower over her. 'Will do. She'll also believe me then—she tends to, well, make fun of me, you know.'

Francesca found that her eyes had adjusted to the gloom, and she discovered that Annette's Jerry, while not handsome, was pleasant-looking despite his size— although that alone might be a little off-putting to an inexperienced girl. But it was all hard muscle, and he had very nice, honest and earnest blue eyes.

She smiled. 'Jerry, even if it's not Annette, there will be one very lucky girl out there for you.'

'As for you, Raefe Stevensen,' she murmured to herself as she climbed into her four-wheel drive, 'we shall see...'

She sprinted across the lawn to the back door of the house, but as an effort to keep dry it was pretty much in vain. She stood on the kitchen porch to wring out her hair and her skirt, then took a deep breath before she marched inside.

But the kitchen was dim and quiet—the whole house was dim and quiet, she discovered, apart from a light showing beneath Raefe's study door. Francesca hesitated, then decided there was no point in delaying things—although she paused to take a towel from the linen cupboard in the passage. After rapping lightly on the door, she opened it without waiting for an answer.

'Come in, Francesca,' he drawled, dropping his pen amongst a litter of papers on the mahogany table. 'Has your frustrated lover left?' He ran a hand idly through his hair.

Francesca rubbed her hair vigorously with the towel and said abruptly, 'There was a misunderstanding. He—'

'So I gathered! Now I must admit I thought he was a little...young for you, but there's no doubt he's a fine physical specimen,' he mused. 'By the way, I wouldn't believe for one moment that he's not after sex with you, so don't be too disappointed,' he added gently, with the kind of gentle satire that cut as lethally as a sharpened arrow.

She took an angry breath, threw the towel to the floor and placed her hands on her hips. 'How can you say those things without at least *listening* to what I have to say?'

Raefe smiled. 'You mean your side of the story, Chessie? Do you think I don't know it? Do you really think you'd be standing there in all your see-through glory if your side of the story wasn't coming through loud and clear?'

Francesca blinked, saw his gaze roam down her body, then looked down herself. And she cursed beneath her breath because her flimsy pearl-grey skirt and pale blouse were moulded to her figure like second skins. Her breasts were outlined as if her bra didn't exist—it was the lightest one she possessed anyway—and the triangle of her light white bikini briefs was hardly concealing either.

Her frustrated gaze rose and clashed with his sardonic almost savagely amused one. Why didn't I stop to think? she berated herself. Why do I *never* stop to think? How to explain so he'll believe I hadn't given it a *thought*?

'You were saying, Chessie?' he drawled.

'I'm saying it was a mistake. In fact, it was a case of—'

'Oh, I believe you,' Raefe murmured, with such patent mockery that her hackles literally rose again. 'Very young men can be a little hard to control, can't they? I mean, once they got the come-on you really need your wits about you, I'm sure. Well...' he shrugged '...that's one scenario.'

Francesca stared at him, her shoulders rigid, her hands still planted firmly on her hips and her eyes darkening to sapphire. 'So you think he followed me here somehow?' she said, in a strangely restrained voice.

'Either that or you summoned him here because you were getting a bit tired of the celibate life you were being forced to lead—how else could it have happened?' he mused mildly. 'I'm only sorry I got a bit worried that you might have bumped into another python when you took such a very long time—sorry from your point of view, that is. It might have saved us this scene.' His gaze roamed her figure again.

'What do you mean?' she said, still in the same voice.

'Saved us from this display of frustration.'

Her mouth hardened. 'Oh?'

'Oh, yes, Chessie.' He was suddenly grim. 'Because I don't intend to help you out.'

'Really?' She took her hands from her hips. 'Not even if I do this?' She started to unbutton her blouse.

He stayed grimly silent while she coolly and carefully released each button from its damp enclosure. She straightened, ran her fingers through her hair and shook it, and slid the blouse off. Then she walked the few steps to the table, pushed aside a pile of papers and perched herself on a corner.

'What do you say now, Mr Stevensen?' She leant towards him, her hands planted on the table, her hair swinging and recovering its toffee-gold colour as it dried, her skin like satin, her breasts firm and proudly cradled in the damp silk and lace of her low-cut bra.

'Go away, Chessie,' he said roughly.

'Getting a bit hard to handle, is it?' she taunted gently, and slipped off the desk to release her skirt. But before her fingers found the zip he stood up violently.

'Mmm...I thought so,' she murmured, not flinching an inch from his murderous gaze, nor allowing the way he stood, taut and almost breathless with control, to escape her cool, ironic gaze.

'Now that's a pity,' she added, and took her hands away from the zip of her skirt as she bent gracefully to pick up her blouse. 'Because I'm about to go to bed—alone, Raefe. Sleep well.'

She was almost at the door before he said, 'One thing, Francesca.'

She stopped, turned and raised an eyebrow at him. 'And what would that be, Mr Stevensen?'

'I've found a married couple—that's why I took Jess to visit our neighbours yesterday. They've been working for them there, but will be happy to transfer to Bramble. Their employers have agreed to sell their property to me, you see.'

'Well, that's wonderful! Thanks for letting me know—when will they be able to move in?'

'In the next couple of days.'

'It gets better and better!' she said cheerfully. 'By the way, that young man you thought I was having such difficulty controlling—that or I'd *summoned* him here—I'd actually never set eyes on him in my life before.'

Their gazes clashed, and Francesca could find no way of masking the anger in her eyes that so belied her tone of voice. But she didn't care.

'No, he's Annette's boyfriend, in fact,' she continued, almost gaily. 'He wasn't aware that she was in Cairns and he mistook me for her because of the rain, the gloom and because I had happened to borrow her raincoat. Goodnight.'

At six o'clock the next morning there was a knock on her door and it opened unceremoniously.

Francesca sat up, rubbed her eyes and pushed her hair back sleepily. It was Raefe—showered, brushed and shaved, wearing his khaki bush shirt and trousers.

'What do you want?' she asked, a shade uncertainly.

His gaze lingered briefly on her French blue camisole top. 'I just came to find out what your plans for the day were,' he said evenly.

'My...?' Comprehension dawned as he looked round searchingly. 'No, I haven't packed. Why? Have you come to escort me off the property personally?'

'Are you planning to leave today?' he countered coolly.

Blue eyes met grey, and Francesca swallowed as she tried to grapple with this in her barely wakened state. Then she remembered all the details of their last encounter and her eyes moved involuntarily to her skirt and blouse, lying in a corner where she'd hurled them the night before. She looked heavenwards exasperatedly.

Unfortunately he'd followed her gaze, and his eyes, as they met hers again, were sardonic.

Sardonic enough to rouse some fighting spirit in her. 'You did ask for it! And if it's something else you're going to choose to disbelieve, why don't you check with Annette? His name is Jericho,' she added bitterly.

A faint smile twisted Raefe's lips. 'Is that a fact? Then my apologies to both you and the unfortunately named young man. Are you planning to walk out on me today, though? Or do you think you got sufficient revenge with your little strip act?'

Francesca moved to cast aside the sheet, but suddenly thought better of it.

'Wise,' he murmured, following her movements. 'You could even find I might be a little hard to control one day.'

'You don't believe a word of it!' she gasped.

'Of course I do,' he said shortly. 'I just don't believe

it was *all* motivated by a desire to make me eat my words. Now is that sufficient to make you reveal your plans for the day, Chessie? I'm sorry to say that I haven't got a lot of time to stand around chatting.'

'You— Do you mean to say you have the absolute nerve to be wondering whether I will stay and care for your daughter, after *all*—? I'm speechless.'

'Listen, Chessie.' He walked over to the bed and towered over her, and there was something suddenly infinitely dangerous about Raefe Stevensen. 'Let's not play any more games. *You* got yourself into this; you started it all. And what I want to know now is whether I can rely on you to look after my most precious possession—the totally innocent party in all this, incidentally—for at least one or two more days.'

'So long,' she said, through stiff, pale lips, 'as that's *it*. And when, *incidentally*, have I not proved totally reliable towards Jess?'

She thought, dimly, through her anger and outrage, that he relaxed slightly. 'Thank you,' was all he said, however, very formally. 'I'm picking Sarah up in Cairns this morning,' he went on. 'She'll be back here this afternoon. We'll be able to work something out then.' And he walked out, closing the door.

Francesca stared at it, then dropped her face into her hands, ground her teeth and burst into tears.

By the time she'd started to make breakfast, Francesca had relaxed slightly. It would help, she reflected, to have someone else around while this deadly war between her and Raefe Stevensen came to an end. Although she hoped Sarah wasn't coming home so suddenly because she hadn't been able to mend her marriage.

But Francesca was still possessed of a cold anger towards the man who continued—indeed relished—believing the worst of her. And, whether Sarah was home temporarily or not, between them they could make arrangements for Jess, because she, Francesca Valentine, was leaving Bramble as soon as possible—even today if Sarah could cope.

'Is it a good day to make biscuits, Chessie?' Jess enquired, coming into the kitchen still flushed from sleep, in her pink and white dotted shortie pyjamas. 'We won't have Daddy under our feet.'

Francesca stared at her—and sighed. And she picked the little girl up to sit her on her lap. 'I guess we won't. Jess...' But she stopped and grimaced as she cradled the slight form against her and rested her chin on Jess's fair curls.

How to tell her she was leaving? How not to damage a child who'd built herself a fairy-tale family out of golliwogs and teddy bears, a child whose aunt might not be coming home to stay, whose mother, to all intents and purposes, might not have existed? Who might be about to have to come to grips with a strange couple ordering her life...

'Yes, it is a good day, Jess. We'll make the best biscuits in the world,' Francesca heard herself say, with a tinge of helplessness.

Sarah arrived at about four o'clock, alone. That was to say a Banyo Air helicopter, not piloted by Raefe, dropped her off and flew off. But it was plain to see this was a transformed Sarah. Gone was that faintly haunted air of sadness. Her eyes sparkled, her cheeks were pink and there was a spring to her step.

'I... Look,' Francesca said, 'Raefe told me. I hope you don't mind. But I only have to look at you to know that...things have worked out well, and I'm glad.'

Sarah hesitated, then she hugged Francesca impulsively. '*Thank* you. Oh, Jess, darling—how are you, my poppet?'

Jess was fine, she told her aunt, and with Chessie's help they'd made some zoo biscuits for afternoon tea, and would she believe it but Mo now had a mate, a girl called Flo, and he was *much* better behaved, and she could do backstroke really well now, and...

'Stop a moment,' Sarah begged. 'This Flo can do backstroke?'

'No, silly—me!' Jess said fondly. 'Come and meet Flo—Chessie *made* her.'

'I'll put the kettle on in the meantime,' Francesca said, seeing Sarah's look of wild speculation. 'You'll probably need a cup of tea.'

They had their tea on the veranda, and after a while Jess wandered off to play.

'So it's been going really well by the sound of it?' Sarah bit into a pink-iced biscuit with a white teddy bear on it.

Francesca paused with her cup half raised to her lips. 'Is that what Raefe said?'

'I haven't seen Raefe today. I haven't seen him since I left.'

'But I thought...' Francesca stopped.

'He was going to collect me this morning in Cairns, but something came up, apparently, so Bill deputised.'

Francesca put her tea down untasted. 'Then does he know? I mean—'

'Does he know my good news? Yes, I called him yesterday afternoon, quite late. He said you were down feeding Bob and Barbara's menagerie—fancy that happening on top of me breaking my wrist! Thank heavens for you, Chessie.'

Francesca picked up her cup again and this time drank some tea. 'Do you think he'll be back tonight? Raefe?'

'No. He's in Brisbane—it's to do with his concession for the airport. There's some hitch, apparently. Someone else has tendered for it, or—don't ask me the details.' Sarah shook her head ruefully. 'In my state of seventh heaven it's all going over the top of my head.' She sobered suddenly. 'I'm afraid I was a bit of a fool.'

'Don't you believe it,' Francesca said warmly. 'It's none of my business, but I'm sure you had your reasons. Are you…home to stay?' she added. 'For any length of time, I mean, obviously.'

'Well, that rather depends on you, once again,' Sarah said wryly. 'Mark and I are planning a second honeymoon.' She blushed attractively. 'I know at my age that seems a bit… But anyway, it's a case of Tahiti, here come a pair of middle-aged second honeymooners! But only if you can put up with Bramble for another fortnight, Chessie.

'What *are* your plans, by the way?' Sarah said anxiously. 'I should have asked you first, but Jess seems so happy and contented and, well, you seem to have fitted in *so* well! But then I keep forgetting who you are!'

He hasn't told her anything... The realisation staggered through Francesca's dazed mind. Let me *think*. I suppose, when he spoke to her yesterday, all was going fairly well. For *us*. But did he know about the second honeymoon then?

'Er—does Raefe know? About your second honeymoon?'

Sarah blushed again. 'No, I didn't actually tell him that. But I can't see that it would be any problem from his point of view—so long as it's OK with you. Of course when I get back—I mean, I realise you can't stay here for ever—we'll have to have a round-table conference of some kind.' She stopped and sighed suddenly.

'If he doesn't marry again soon, I'm thinking that Jess will either have to come and live with us—I know Mark wouldn't mind—or, if Raefe can't bear to be parted from her, *he* might have to move south. At least he could get decent help so much more easily there!'

Francesca studied Sarah's earnest face, then she looked around and tried to imagine Raefe leaving Bramble—and what would happen to Banyo Air?

She said abruptly, 'What did happen to Jess's mother?'

Sarah looked surprised. 'Hasn't he told you?'

'No.'

Sarah sighed. 'I was hoping it would be getting easier for him—at least to talk about. It's been, well, I guess it's eighteen months now since Olivia... They might have been made for each other, you know. Which was strange, in a way, because she wasn't glamorous, and Raefe's been pursued by glamorous women ever since I can remember! But Olivia was a vet—that's how they came to meet. She specialised in cattle.'

Francesca's eyes widened.

'Not that she wasn't attractive, in a lean, boyish sort of way,' Sarah continued. 'She just didn't care much about clothes and so on. But they just clicked—they were lovely together. And it was the ideal sort of partnership because she had plenty to occupy herself with here and she had the same sort of daredevil streak in her Raefe has. He taught her to fly.'

'So—why did she leave him?' Francesca heard herself ask.

Sarah blinked. 'She didn't. She was killed in a car accident.'

Francesca's mouth fell open. 'Then why,' she whispered, 'is there no…is there *nothing* around to remember her by?'

'That's because of Jess,' Sarah said sadly. 'She was in the car too, although she wasn't seriously injured, and every time Olivia was mentioned or she saw a photo of her, or saw her clothes or anything, she became so absolutely distraught and suffered such shocking nightmares, we decided—with medical advice too—to remove all reminders for the time being. They say that eventually she'll be able to remember her mother without the trauma.'

There was a long silence. Then Francesca said very quietly, 'I wish…someone had told me this sooner.'

'But you've been so marvellous with Jess!' Sarah objected. 'I mean, I'm sure you couldn't have been any better even if you had known.'

'Perhaps,' Francesca murmured. 'I haven't been so marvellous with her father, though.'

CHAPTER SEVEN

'I—I DIDN'T know what to do,' Francesca said the next morning. 'She was so happy. She said she could go with a clear conscience if she knew I was here for Jess—I didn't know what to do,' she repeated.

They were on the beach. Once again Raefe had arrived very early by four-wheel drive, and once again he'd made straight for the beach. Francesca, just up herself and the only one to be so, had seen him.

She'd pulled on a pair of shorts and a halter-top, washed her face, dragged a brush through her hair and, taking a deep breath, had walked outside. She'd caught up with him just as he'd reached the enclosure gate and told him abruptly that she needed to talk to him.

His eyes had narrowed, his hands had stilled on the buttons of his shirt, then he'd suggested they walk for a bit.

'You didn't mention the couple from Tallai—the neighbouring property?'

'No. Well, no,' Francesca said as they walked side by side in the sunrise. A dawn chorus of Torres Strait pigeons in the trees fringing the beach greeted the day with their strange hoo-hoo call. 'Sarah didn't mention them so I assumed you hadn't told her—anything,' she added rather drily.

'No, I didn't. I...' He paused and frowned. 'Like you, I suppose, I didn't want to dent her happiness in the slightest. But why didn't she tell me about this second honeymoon?'

'I think she's a bit embarrassed and shy—she maintains that she's middle-aged.' They looked at each other and smiled wryly. Francesca added after a moment, 'You should see her now, though. She looks just lovely.'

Raefe stopped walking and stared out to sea. After a few moments, Francesca sank down onto a smooth log and watched the sun rise, turning the water from pale grey to apricot. And when Raefe didn't move she transferred her gaze to him, where he stood half turned away from her, with his hands shoved into his pockets and a delicious little breeze lifting his fair hair off his forehead.

He seemed totally unaware of her regard and deep in thought, and her heart started to beat heavily in the way she was coming to know well. Because, however much this man contrived to infuriate her, at the same time he attracted her deeply—she could no longer deny it.

Not that I've tried to deny it for a while, she mused. I just didn't realise the strength of it. I didn't anticipate that Sarah saying something about him marrying again would hit me like a hurricane and make me *ache* to think it couldn't be me. But why couldn't it be me? If I told him the truth, laid to rest all the rumours and the gossip, didn't get carried away and make out I'm as bad as I'm painted...

She closed her eyes and clenched her teeth.

But what would be the point? she thought wearily after a moment. The real problem is—could I ever take the place of the wife he loved so much? If I couldn't, I think I know myself well enough to know that it would frustrate me unbearably. And he must have loved her very much. It explains so many things…

'Chessie?'

She stared and focused on him. 'Sorry, did you say something?' she murmured.

'No, but you looked…strangely sad,' he said slowly, and with a frown in his eyes.

'Did I?' She shrugged and gathered her defences. 'Perhaps it was a trick of the light. What will we do?'

He hesitated, then came to sit beside her on the log, resting his elbows on his knees and clasping his hands between them. 'I seem to be thoroughly jinxed at the moment,' he said ruefully. 'First Sarah, then Bob, on top of all the problems of being a single parent are thoroughly exacerbated by living in the back of beyond. What I really need is a wife.'

Francesca winced inwardly, but managed to say composedly, 'She would have my sympathies if those were the only reasons you needed her.'

'You're right, of course, Chessie. It was a stupid thing to say. Be that as it may, what we'll do rather depends on you.'

'Are you asking me to stay?' she said abruptly.

'Yes, Chessie, once again I'm asking you to stay.' The self-directed irony in his voice was plain to hear.

'What about the couple from Tallai?'

He moved his shoulders restlessly. 'They're coming, but I wasn't really intending to foist them on Jess cold turkey, if you know what I mean.'

'Until I enraged you the night before last?' she suggested after a moment, with a certain amount of cynicism, but went on before he could speak. 'But you must have had some plan—that didn't include me,' she added deliberately.

He glanced at her and smiled slightly. 'The plan I had didn't include Sarah going to Tahiti on a second honeymoon,' he said wryly. 'I was hoping that even if she and Mark did make it up she'd come up, or both of them, for a transition period, so to speak.'

'I could do that,' Francesca said quietly. 'But it's up to you. The longer I'm here, the harder it's going to be for Jess,' she added, and felt a shaft of guilt pass through her that caused her to jump up suddenly and pace a few steps agitatedly. I did start this, she thought miserably. Not that I was to know how hard it would be for *me*, but Jess…

'Chessie, I'm as much to blame,' he said quietly, from right behind her.

She turned convulsively. 'No—sometimes I just don't stop to *think*.'

He stared down at her. 'Nor, I'm afraid, do I—'

'And you see,' she went on, overriding him tautly, 'I didn't *know*, and if I've offended you with any of my behaviour I apologise.'

'Didn't know what?' he said after a moment.

'I thought—I assumed,' she said stiffly, 'that your wife must have left you.' She saw him tense involuntarily then deliberately relax.

'Why did you assume that?'

'I…' She gestured a little helplessly. 'There was no evidence that you'd ever *had* a wife. And you treated me right from the start with such—such cynicism, I couldn't believe that it was only based on…seeing me in the social pages.' She couldn't help the trace of bitterness that crept into her voice, but made herself add with honesty, 'Or the fact that sometimes the worst of my father's arrogance comes out in me.'

'But now you know differently—how?'

'Sarah told me yesterday. I asked her,' Francesca said bleakly.

'I see.'

'There's no reason why I shouldn't know—is there?' she said, after a long, strangely tense pause.

'No, of course not,' he said briefly, but somehow Francesca didn't believe him. And then, quite suddenly, she knew why, and although it was only a confirmation of what she'd already told herself it came like a blow to the heart.

She understood, with no hope of there being any two ways about it, that Raefe Stevensen couldn't bear to share the memory of his beloved Olivia with another woman—least of all her. Was it because she'd forced him to face the fact that while he might not love another woman he could still want her physically?

As the thought took root there seemed to be only one thing to do—run. As if to escape it, as if to… She whirled on her heel and did just that—ran away from him and the horror of what she'd done, ran up the beach away from the homestead as if pursued by all the demons in hell.

She heard him swear, then start after her, but when, inevitably, he caught her she fought like a demented tigress and managed to break away from him. This time he dived after her in a classic rugby tackle about the knees and felled her onto the soft sand, then imprisoned her by the simple expedient of lying on top of her with his arms firmly around her.

'History repeats itself,' he said softly, when her energy finally gave out and she lay still and panting for breath beneath him. 'Although I got that bit wrong, didn't I?'

'If you're talking about Jericho, *yes*,' she gasped. 'But that wasn't the only bit— Will you let me go?'

'No.' But he rolled off her, although he still kept her firmly clasped in his arms. 'Not until you tell me what that was all about, anyway.'

'I'm telling you *nothing*,' she shot back through her teeth. 'And if you don't let me go I'll bite and kick and scratch—'

'You've already done some of those things,' he pointed out ruefully. 'But it's getting you no-where—other than exhausting yourself.'

Francesca made one more desperate effort to free herself, only to have him laugh quietly at her, then drawl, 'I can see there's only one remedy—this. And don't bite, Chessie,' he added wryly. 'It's a bit undignified, surely?'

And he ran one hand through her hair, pulled her closer with the other, and started to kiss her.

Fight *this*, Chessie, she told herself dimly. If nothing else, fight this... But it was too late—she had exhausted herself—and with a sob of pure frustration she lay still beneath his hands and mouth.

He kissed her brow and her throat, pausing only to dust some sand from her cheek. He caressed her hip and thigh in a slow, rhythmic and increasingly intimate exploration that gradually caused a tingling of her nerve-ends and brought a taut, lovely sense of expectancy to her. It caused her nipples to ache and flower, caused her to feel herself grow warm and wet with desire. And only then did he kiss her mouth.

When she was helpless beneath this sensual onslaught, not only from what his hands were doing to her but also the feel of his body against hers, the warmth and strength of it—only then did he start to kiss her properly.

And she knew she was lost when her lips parted willingly and she moved against him with a kind of hunger.

Ten minutes later she sat on a grassy outcrop beside the beach and watched as Raefe swam vigorously. Then she looked away, down at her hands clasped between her knees, feeling hollow and tormented because she had stopped on the brink and he had accepted it.

But it hadn't been what she'd wanted to do at all, and it was only the fact that she'd never been made love to that had given her strength to achieve this reluctant victory.

'Chessie?'

She looked up to see him standing in front of her in his underpants, drying himself perfunctorily with his shirt.

'Yes?' she whispered.

'You'd feel better for a swim too.'

'Would I?' She smiled mechanically. 'Thanks, but I'll make do with the proverbial cold shower.'

He dropped down to the grass verge beside her and pulled on his shirt. 'It wouldn't work—do you know why it wouldn't work?'

'You and I?' she said after a long pause. 'Probably—you don't have to give me a catalogue.'

'*You* stopped,' he said after a brief hesitation.

'And if I hadn't?'

She wasn't looking at him but out to sea, nor did she move as the silence lengthened, and he took his time to study her—the lovely line of her throat and the smooth curves of her shoulders just brushed by that glorious hair, the sweep of her golden legs which she'd pulled up and clasped with her hands.

The knowledge, he thought with brutal honesty, that her breasts lay beneath whatever she wore like the perfect, tantalising fruit he'd first thought them tormented him awake and asleep, as did the slenderness of her waist, the curves of her hips, the narrow elegance of her hands and feet.

He found himself wondering suddenly, for the first time, if she knew just how beautiful she was, and just how much self-control he'd had to exert over these past days. He wondered it with a frown in his eyes, and the odd feeling that he'd missed something.

'Would *you*? Have stopped if I hadn't?' She looked around, catching him by surprise, and her eyes were a breathtaking deep blue.

He grimaced and acknowledged that he might not have been able to. 'I don't know,' he heard himself say. 'Not if you were willing. Chessie—well, we've already decided I'm not a block of wood, haven't we?'

He heard her breath expel sharply, and knew with

an unexpected pang that he'd hurt her. But she said nothing, only looked away to sea again. And that surprised him as well. He sighed inwardly and said, 'Perhaps we should not so much catalogue anything, but discuss why it wouldn't work.'

'I know why,' she responded briefly.

'Do you? Want to tell me?' he said quietly.

'No.'

'Even if I were to tell *you* that it wasn't purely an idle remark about my needing a wife?'

That brought her up short, he noticed, with a strange kind of satisfaction.

'What do you mean?' She turned to him again, her eyes wide.

'I mean it crossed my mind that you could solve all my problems in one fell swoop.'

Her lips parted and she could only stare at him.

'But,' he went on, 'in the next breath it occurred to me that this was Francesca Valentine I was having these thoughts about. Not a girl who would be happy tied to a cattle station for the rest of her life. Not a girl— Look at me, Chessie,' he commanded softly, and made himself go on the best way he knew how, the only way to hurt her the least in the long run. 'Not a girl you could offer second best to. A girl, in other words, who deserved to be loved whole-heartedly.'

There was a heart-stopping silence. Then she said huskily, 'You don't really believe that about me, do you?'

'Which bit?'

'That I deserve anything. You've made that plain enough.'

It was his turn to look away briefly and force himself to concentrate. 'Whatever else I may have accused you of or suspected you of, Chessie, there's a side to you that is pure gold. The side that made you take a motherless, traumatised little girl and bring her ease and warmth and companionship in a way that's been…lovely to see.'

Francesca stared at him, then looked down at her knees.

'But,' he went on, 'do you know what the real appeal of these last weeks has been for you, Chessie?'

'No. What?' she said, barely audibly, and suddenly laid her cheek on her knees.

'What may have been the first taste of normal family life for you—or what could be a normal family life.'

She said after an age, 'Of course, you're right. About that.' Then she sat up straight. 'Not to be confused with anything else. It's all right, Raefe, I know you're trying to let me down lightly, and don't think I'm not grateful. But that doesn't get us much further forward. I—'

'I spoke to your father the other day, Chessie,' he said abruptly.

Sheer shock held her speechless suddenly. Then she found her voice, but it came out strangled and amazed. '*Why?*'

'I didn't want to be accused of keeping you here against your will—and nor was I wrong. For whatever reason, he was not about to put up with you disappearing off the face of the earth, to all intents and purposes, for much longer.'

Francesca laughed coldly. 'Don't tell me he was about to mount a rescue campaign!'

'As a matter of fact he was.'

'Are you serious?'

'Yes. He…' He paused, then shrugged. 'He was thoroughly exasperated to think, amongst other things, that you might not realise how open to exploitation you are.'

'And you managed to set his mind at rest?' she said caustically.

'Not entirely. He either wants you home by the end of the week or he wants to speak to you personally by then.'

'You *must* have made an impression—why are you telling me this now?'

'Because I very nearly blotted my copybook,' he replied drily. 'And because you seem to doubt that I could have any regard for you other than as a means to relieve my physical frustrations.'

'I…I don't understand.'

'Don't you?' He looked at her ironically. 'Why would I care what becomes of Frank Valentine's daughter? Why would I bother to tell him that he really should take better care of you—of your mental well-being—if I didn't…if I didn't owe you a very real debt, Chessie? But it's one I can't repay any other way, because I…' He stopped.

Can't forget Olivia. Francesca didn't say it, but it was there between them as if she had spoken. But the thing that hurt most, she thought, was that he still held a mistaken view of her. He still couldn't see that this person who had looked after Jess was the real Chessie, not someone who had fallen under the brief spell of a kind of domestic harmony she hadn't known before.

That she was the kind of person who could easily give away the bright lights and the social pages, had never had much time for them anyway, and had been a victim of her father's flamboyant lifestyle if anything... But then again, what difference does it make? she asked herself. Whatever he thinks, I'd only be dashing myself against the memory of Olivia all the time.

'Raefe...' She paused and steepled her fingers to her mouth for an instant, fighting for composure and the right tone. 'Thanks for that, and you don't owe me anything. Not many people would be immune to Jess. But I think you'd better send Sarah to Tahiti with a clear conscience and you'd better arrange for the couple from Tallai to move in as soon as possible.

'I'll do all in my power to fade away with as little pain as possible. She is only seven. Why don't you plan a few treats for her? You could take her to visit the School of the Air base in Cairns. And she would probably love to have a puppy or a kitten.'

'Chessie—'

But she'd had enough. 'No. It's all been said, Raefe.' She stood up lithely and stared down at him for a moment. 'Don't lose any sleep over it.'

He watched her walk away without making any attempt to follow her. Watched her straight shoulders, her swinging arms and hair, the rounded curve of her buttocks as they moved up and down beneath the white cotton of her shorts, then switched his gaze away deliberately and cursed beneath his breath.

Cursed himself primarily, but also fate for choosing to send the beautiful enigma that was Francesca Valentine across his path...

'I had a mummy once,' Jess said. 'Did you ever have one, Chessie?'

They were at the breakfast table, all of them, that same morning, but while Francesca, Raefe and Sarah were lingering over coffee, discussing Tahiti, Jess had finished and was paging through a picture book.

They all froze.

Until Francesca leant over to see what had prompted this in Jess, and saw her studying a picture of a family—a mother and father, and two children.

'Yes, I did,' Francesca said slowly. 'But she—she went to heaven when I was just a little girl, Jess.'

'So did mine. She's with the angels now. I could show you a picture, only Daddy put them all away—didn't you?' She turned to Raefe.

'I...I could get them out again,' he said, in a voice curiously unlike his own.

'Oh, good, then I *can* show Chessie. Now come on, Mo and Flo—' she unhooked the monkeys who'd shared her chair-back during breakfast '—we're going to check up on those gollies—I just hope they've been good!' And she scampered off happily.

Sarah had sudden tears streaming down her cheeks. 'They said it was only a matter of time, didn't they, Raefe?'

But as they stared at each other, brother and sister, it was plain that Raefe couldn't trust his voice, and he got up and walked outside. Francesca watched him go and found she had tears in her eyes too.

And, later in the day, that was how she was able to put a face to the shadowy figure that had lurked in her mind almost since she'd first met Raefe Stevensen. But, not only that, it was how she came to put the last nail in the coffin of her dreams.

For Olivia Stevensen, captured in a silver frame with her blonde hair blowing about her small face, her slim form carelessly dressed in a pair of khaki trousers and a bush shirt, was laughing up at Raefe with adoration in her eyes, as he was laughing down at her. But that wasn't all. She was so like Jess it was almost breathtaking.

Somehow or other Francesca was able to put the photo down steadily on the cabinet it had come from, and marshal her resources to speak normally to both Raefe and Jess.

'She's lovely. I wish I had a photo to show you of my mother, Jess, but I can tell you about her anyway. She had the same colour hair as mine—she used to say it might get me into a lot of bother and she wasn't wrong! Isn't it funny that I should remember that? But I do,' she added slowly.

'Why?' Jess asked. 'There's nothing wrong with your hair.'

Out of the corner of her eye, Francesca saw Raefe relax somewhat, and knew that he must have been dreading this moment in case it went awfully wrong. But Jess only looked enquiring.

'Well, you see, sugar, it might be more golden-brown now, but it started out a bit red. And redheads can be people who get into a lot of trouble because they...er...'

'Can be strong-willed.' Raefe took over. 'And have bad tempers, Jess.'

'But Chessie's not like that,' Jess objected.

'No, you're right—she's not,' her father agreed gravely, then hesitated. 'Shall we leave this photo out now?'

'Yes, please,' Jess said. 'Then I can bring my toys in and show them. Chessie, we mustn't forget to feed Bob and Barbara's animals—shall I get your car keys?' And she ran off without waiting for a reply.

Leaving Francesca and Raefe alone.

'I'm sorry—so very sorry,' Francesca said, barely audibly. 'She is lovely.'

'And it seems I owe you another debt,' he replied.

'No. I'm sure they were right. It was only a matter of time—and don't worry. I'll keep an eye on Jess in case there are any repercussions.' And she left the lounge quietly.

There weren't.

Jess went to bed serenely that night, and it was left to Francesca to toss and turn in the hot darkness as she grappled with the knowledge that while time might have worked in Jess's favour it was going to do the opposite for Raefe. It was going to give him a constant, living reminder in the form of his daughter.

The next few days were filled with comings and goings. Sarah left, and a day and a half later the Forsters arrived from Tallai.

'Look, I think we'll do this gradually,' Raefe said, the morning of their arrival.

Francesca glinted an enquiring look at him. He'd

asked her to come into his study after breakfast and to bring their coffee with her. It was an overcast, hot day, as steamy as a Turkish bath.

'Sit down,' he murmured, and turned the overhead fan on, placing paperweights on the piles of paper on the table.

Francesca sat, and was visited by the most acute recollection of virtually disrobing herself in this very room a few nights ago—it was the first time she'd been in it since. Consequently she said, 'You were saying?' rather abruptly.

Raefe, in khaki shorts and a yellow T-shirt that was already clinging to his back, sat down and reached for his coffee-cup. 'I think I'll put the Forsters down in Bob and Barbara's cottage for a couple of days. By the way, they go by the names of Pete and Milly. Milly can come up every day and take over the housekeeping from you and get to know Jess—gradually. And I thought they could have their evening meals with us, so Jess can get to know Pete as well.'

Francesca sipped her coffee. 'Sounds like good thinking to me,' she replied eventually. 'Bob and Barbara wouldn't mind—how are they, by the way?'

'Bob's out of hospital now, and they're all crammed into Annette's flat. But I've arranged for them to have a month's holiday at Mission Beach, just south of Cairns. Annette will be able to spend weekends with them. As well as the young man with the unfortunate name,' he added with a fleeting grin.

'That was his mother,' Francesca responded wryly. 'She also told him faint heart never won fair lady.'

'I gather the Browns are discovering that.'

'Damn.' Francesca grimaced. 'I told him to go slowly.'

'Did you?'

'Well, she is only eighteen.'

Raefe sat back. 'Where were you when you were eighteen, Chessie?'

Francesca blinked and thought back. 'At a finishing school.'

'Here? In Australia?'

'No, overseas—in France.'

'Did you learn much there?'

'I learnt to ski and speak French, and how to conduct myself as a lady.' A faint smile played across her mouth. 'Not that they were entirely successful there. In fact at one stage they were all set to send me home. I'm not sure how much it cost my father to make them change their minds,' she reflected.

'What did you do?' Raefe asked after a moment.

'Well, I didn't have a flaming affair with the ski instructor or the dancing master, if that's what you're thinking.' She tossed her hair. 'I simply went walkabout several times.'

'Just—took off?'

'Uh-huh. It wasn't my idea to be there in the first place, you see. So I thought that if I *had* to be in France I might as well see a bit more of it—the bits I wanted to see as opposed to the bits they wanted to show me on carefully shepherded tours.'

'What bits were those?'

She tipped a hand. 'Places I'd read about.'

'Off the beaten track?' he suggested.

'Yes.' A sudden far-away glint lit her eyes. 'It was lovely.'

'Meanwhile the whole country was being scoured for you?'

Francesca came back with a faintly rueful look. 'I guess so—but have you never read about places that have so captured your imagination you almost can't help yourself?'

'Yes, like you, I set off to find some of them too—only I didn't have to run away to do it.'

'Sarah told me.' Francesca looked amused. 'Was it fun flying a sheikh and his harem about the world?'

'It had its enlivening moments. Harems can be a handful.'

They laughed together, then Francesca said curiously, 'Were you allowed to see inside any of them?'

'Only on pain of death.'

'Seriously?'

'Well, perhaps not, but it wasn't a wise thing to do—if not from one's own point of view, which could result in one meeting with a nasty little accident, then certainly from the ladies'.'

Francesca was silent. 'I just can't imagine it.'

'Just as well—I feel quite strongly that you would not be at all suited to a harem, Chessie.'

'I know,' Francesca said drily, without thinking.

'Know?' He raised an eyebrow at her.

'I mean—well, how many women do you know who would?'

'Point taken,' he replied, and a strange little silence followed as they eyed each other—Francesca with a tinge of hostility that she couldn't quite hide, Raefe with a frown in his eyes.

Then Francesca stood up with an air of decision about her. 'Is there anything you want me to do?'

'Such as?'

'Such as—' she gestured impatiently '—preparing for this Milly and Pete in any way?'

He stood up. 'No, thanks. They're quite capable of seeing to anything that needs doing down at the Browns' cottage. Chessie—'

But whatever he would have said was destined to be unknown as the VHF radio came to life.

'*Sécurité, sécurité, sécurité,*' the disembodied voice said, over some static. 'This is Townsville Radio, Victor India Tango. Hello, all ships, this is Townsville Radio. We have a cyclone alert issued by the Bureau of Meteorology at zero six hundred hours this morning. A low-pressure system has developed overnight in the Coral Sea...'

Raefe grabbed a pencil and began to make notes. Francesca watched and listened with growing disbelief, but only spoke when the broadcast was finished. 'Is it coming this way? Where is it?'

'Still a few hundred miles off the coast north-east of us, and stationary at the moment, but if it develops and travels south-west, who knows?' he said wearily, and tossed the pencil down. 'The last bloody thing I need at the moment!'

CHAPTER EIGHT

'WILL we have to evacuate?' Francesca asked.

'Not at this stage—cyclones are notoriously unpredictable. They can double back on their tracks, change direction, et cetera. Nor is it a full-blown one yet, but we'll have to be prepared. And not only for destructive gale-force winds—once they cross the coast they tend to degenerate into rain depressions which mean floods.'

'We've only just—' Francesca stopped.

'As you say. Look, if you want to get out while the going's good, I won't hold it against you.'

'That's very kind of you but I'm not a coward.' She eyed him coldly.

'Chessie...' He drew in an exasperated breath. 'I'm not *suggesting* that. Your father, for one thing, would—'

'You just leave my father to me, Raefe,' she advised. 'Would I be right in surmising that you'll be stretched to the limit protecting both Banyo Air and Bramble Downs from a cyclone if it happens?'

'I...' He paused, his grey eyes narrowing. 'Why do I get the feeling anything I say is going to be taken down and used as evidence—against me?'

'Because I'm right, aren't I?' she informed him coolly. 'Look, if you're worried I'm going to take advantage of you at the same time, perish the thought,' she said gently. 'I—'

'Take advantage of me as in *how*?' he asked through his teeth.

'As in catching you off your guard and sweeping you off your feet!' she murmured, with a glimmer of amusement in her blue eyes. 'Or just plain seducing you.'

He swore.

'Dear me—you should have let me finish,' she remonstrated, her lips twitching. 'I'm over all that, is what I was going to say. I do hope you believe me, Raefe. I've got the feeling you're going to need your wits about you for a few days. In the meantime I'll do all I can to help.' And she walked out of the study, closing the door gently behind her.

She leant back against it for a moment and clenched her fists, then sighed deeply. Why do I do it? she wondered. But it occurred to her that this time she hadn't acted with the inborn arrogance she might never be able to subdue completely, but out of a sense of self-protection for her battered heart…

Nor was she entirely surprised when he retaliated, but that came much later in the day.

In the event it turned out to be an uncomfortable sort of day. Pete and Milly Forster arrived and took over the Browns' cottage, and Jess retreated somewhat.

To give her her due, Milly Forster couldn't be blamed for it. She was a comfortably plump, middle-aged woman with a sense of humour, and she confided to Francesca that she had four grown-up children and seven grandchildren. She didn't make a fuss of Jess, and seemed content to allow the little girl to take her time over the process of their getting to know each other.

Francesca couldn't help approving this tactic, nor could she help thinking that Raefe had chosen wisely—Milly Forster was both sensible and kindly, as well as obviously experienced with children. But it hurt her, nevertheless, to see Jess retreating into her shell, as if she had an intimation of what was to come.

On top of this, the hot, overcast mugginess of the day plus the thought of a shrieking cyclone somewhere out to sea waiting to pounce on them was harder on the nerves than Francesca had anticipated. But she forced herself to make good her promise to help, and in a two-pronged effort she and Milly worked side by side through the afternoon, checking the cold room for supplies they might need, checking torches, batteries and candles, and checking the house and surrounds for anything that could become a missile in gale-force winds.

The effort was two-pronged in that it also helped Milly to familiarise herself with Bramble homestead and its workings. They rang through with the list of supplies to Raefe, who was at the airfield, co-ordinating that end of things, and he would fly them home with him that evening.

It turned out that Milly and Pete were old hands at cyclones, and by the time they had dinner—she, Milly and Jess alone; Pete had spent most of his day organising things down at the cattle yards—every window was taped across, to prevent it from shattering, and every garden chair, dustbin lid and so on was either tied down or stowed away.

'Probably won't even hit—nine times out of ten they don't,' Milly said, wiping the sweat off her brow. 'But you can never be sure. She's a quiet little thing, isn't she?' She nodded at Jess.

'Sometimes. Do we know where this cyclone is?'

'Pete knows. He and Raefe have kept in touch. I don't reckon it'll hit tonight. I must say—' she smiled ruefully '—it's not every day you start a new job in these conditions.'

Francesca felt a stab of guilt as she realised she'd probably been preoccupied and withdrawn herself. 'You've been great,' she said warmly. 'You've hardly had a minute to yourself, you've had to take over someone else's cottage and you've barely had time to drop your bags, let alone unpack!'

But Milly said philosophically, 'That's the way we do things up here. Although now dinner's done I might go down to the cottage, if you don't mind. Raefe's due in shortly, so you don't need to worry—there's no way he'd leave you and young Jess alone for long. Will you be all right?'

'Fine. Thanks!'

'That's Daddy,' Jess said, sitting up in Francesca's lap.

They were in the lounge reading a book, and, although Jess was having difficulty keeping her eyes open, it was plain she was determined to do so until her father arrived home.

'Yes, sugar,' Francesca murmured, and touched her lips to the curly fair head in the moment before Jess slipped off her lap and ran to greet Raefe as he walked into the room.

'Daddy, Daddy—I thought you were never coming!' Jess said with a hint of tears in her voice, causing Raefe, at the same time as he swung her up into his arms, to glance across at Francesca with a frown of enquiry in his eyes.

'Just a slightly unsettling day,' Francesca murmured.

'Well, Miss Muffet, here I am—you should know your old dad never stays away for long!'

'You're not old, Daddy,' Jess said lovingly, and she snuggled against him, obviously content again. Half an hour later, after sitting with him as he ate his kept-hot dinner, she was quite happy to be put to bed.

Francesca came out of Jess's room and closed the door softly—to encounter Raefe walking down the passage with a cup of coffee in his hands. He raised an eyebrow at her.

'Asleep,' she said. 'It's probably this heat and awful uncertainty that's as much to blame as anything,' she added, and wiped her hand across her clammy brow. Her hair was damp at the roots, and perspiration was trickling down between her breasts.

'Oh, we're quite safe tonight,' he said, and turned into the lounge.

Francesca frowned, then followed him into the lamplit room. 'What do you mean?'

'I mean it's gone out to sea again and it's travelling south-east—away from us in other words.'

'And you didn't see fit to tell me this as soon as

you got home?' she asked ominously, putting her hands on her hips.

He cast himself down onto the settee and regarded her wryly. 'You look like an avenging angel, Chessie,' he drawled. 'Albeit a slightly hot and bothered one.'

'Don't— Why didn't you *say* so?'

'I thought you knew.'

'No, I didn't know. I mean—well, obviously I knew it wasn't about to hit right now, but—'

'Obviously,' he agreed drily. 'Why are you over-reacting like this, Chessie? You must know I'd never leave Jess alone in any danger.'

'*You* were the one who told me how unpredictable they could be. *I'm* the one who has spent the best part of her day taping things down, tying things up and so on!'

'Very wise,' he commented. 'You never know and you can't be too prepared. Are you, by any chance…' he paused to study her thoughtfully '…finding yourself not quite as brave as you first thought, Chessie?'

That did it. She stepped forward, bent down and slapped his face. Unfortunately, the angle robbed the blow of most of its sting and—disastrously—after a frozen split second gave him the opportunity to tumble her down into his lap. And the opportunity to silence her protestations before they left her lips by placing his mouth on hers and commencing to kiss her brutally.

'You…promised!' she gasped when he allowed her to come up for air.

'No, *you* promised, Chessie,' he corrected her grimly, gathering both her wrists in one hand as she struggled to get free. 'Stay still,' he warned, and she couldn't doubt that he meant it.

All the same, as she subsided she said bitterly, 'Well, you started this!'

'I hesitate to contradict you, but *you* started it—surely you know by now that to slap a man's face is more than likely going to get you kissed in retaliation?'

The terrible unfairness of this struck her speechless, then she forgot his warning and sat up, although still in his arms, to say passionately and incredulously, 'It never crossed my mind! How dare you? I was simply responding t-to—' she stammered in her anger '—to one of your interminable insults!'

'Which one was that?' He raised an eyebrow and she could see amusement creeping into his grey eyes. 'I don't recall—'

'You called me a coward. Well, as good as,' she amended.

'No, I didn't,' he replied. 'I merely intimated that—'

'That I was not as brave as I might like to think I am,' she finished deliberately for him. 'If that's not— If that was not *intended* as an insult, then I'm a Dutchman!'

They stared at each other. Then he let her wrists go suddenly and smiled unexpectedly. 'All right. You were so sure this morning that you could cope with anything, perhaps I *was* indulging in a bit of derision—for which I apologise.'

Francesca eyed him haughtily—and sighed abruptly. 'It's not that I'm scared so much; it's this awful waiting. And to see you going around as cool as a cucumber, as well as Milly and Pete, is very aggravating, if you must know,' she added candidly.

'There are several reasons for that, Chessie. We're used to it. We generally get a couple of these cyclone alerts a year and you learn to live with them. I admit, at times it's frustrating, having to go through all the motions, but you can bet your bottom dollar the one time you ignore an alert is the time it's going to hit. By the way, I don't remember being as cool as a cucumber when we discussed this this morning,' he reminded her.

'You were distinctly annoyed, as I recall correctly.'

'So you see.'

She shrugged and looked at her hands desolately. 'I still think you could have told me.'

'I'm sorry,' he said, barely audibly, after an age, and put his fingers beneath her chin to tilt her face towards him.

She resisted looking at him for a moment, then lifted her lashes, but something had already told her what she would see—naked desire in those grey eyes that could be so cool, so damningly amused, so cynical…

She took an uncertain breath and whispered, 'No, I should go…'

'Go, Chessie?' he murmured, his lids heavy now. 'There's no place to go. Besides, I need to make amends.' And he drew her against him and started to kiss her again.

So different this time, she marvelled on one plane

of her mind. So lovely—why am I not resisting? *How* to resist? Don't be foolish, Francesca Valentine. There's always a way to resist, even if only by not responding. But I am responding. Does that mean I haven't given up hope entirely? The hope that I can change things?

Then she thought no more for several minutes as she gave herself over to the sheer rapture of his mouth on hers, his hands on her body, slipping beneath her top and touching her breasts until she trembled. She made a strange little sound in her throat, and slid her hand up the long, strong lines of his throat.

That was when he stopped. Not hastily, but with an unmistakable sort of finality as he eased her away from him gently, so her head was lying against his shoulder. And when her breathing steadied she could see that he was staring fixedly across the room. She turned her head and knew immediately why he had stopped—not because of anything she had done, as she'd first thought.

Had he forgotten? she asked herself. Had Olivia's photo been put away for so long that he hadn't remembered it was now sitting on the cabinet, only feet from them, looking down on them?

Then he closed his eyes, and there were lines of pain etched beside his mouth. His hands left her body—and she slid off his lap, got to her feet and slipped out of the room.

She woke the next morning a bare instant after she'd fallen asleep—or so it seemed. Woke to the sound of wind and heavy rain. The cyclone, she thought groggily. Don't tell me it's coming after all.

* * *

The only good thing that could be said about that day in particular and cyclones in general was that one's mind was taken off all else.

Raefe called a council of war in the kitchen, which Milly and Pete attended as well as the three stockhands employed. 'According to all reports it's going to cross the coast here.' He indicated a spot south of Bramble on the large-scale map rolled out on the kitchen table. 'If it stays on that course we'll only get the side-effects of it, but that can still mean destructive winds.'

'Sounds a bit destructive now, if you know what I mean,' one of the stockmen drawled.

They all paused to listen to the wind, which was indeed howling—tearing at the bougainvillea on the walls of the house and bending small trees almost in half, as well as blowing the teeming rain nearly horizontal.

'About thirty-five knots, I'd estimate—expect it to get worse,' Raefe said briefly. 'Now, just in case it changes course and crosses here, does everybody know the game-plan?'

They all nodded.

'OK. The main thing is to keep Jess calm and occupied—Chessie, don't you worry about anything else; leave that to us.'

'Will do,' she said quietly. 'Has she ever—? I suppose she has.'

'Yes, she's been through a few blows, but this may be the worst.'

It was a long day, but Francesca suggested to Jess that, seeing as they couldn't get outside, it might be a good time to spring-clean the whole playroom. So that was what they did.

Fortunately the playroom faced away from the wind, so they weren't worried by seeping water, as was becoming a problem in the rest of the house, and could have a window open.

Once they'd done that, they went through Jess's 'family' one by one. Francesca got out Sarah's sewing box and patched up any seams coming adrift. They replaced a couple of button eyes and then brushed all the furry coats, washed and ironed any removable clothes and did the same for the entire dolls' wardrobe.

'There,' Jess said finally at about three o'clock in the afternoon. 'Don't they all look lovely?'

Francesca agreed, then put the back of her hand to her forehead.

'Something wrong?' Raefe asked, coming in at that moment.

She took her hand away and said briefly, 'I'm OK.' But in truth she had a pounding headache, and the sound of the wind was a sheer torment to her nerves. The way the house seemed literally to shake on its foundations was frightening, and the odd bumps and thumps and tearing of timber she heard the same.

'It's easing,' he said abruptly. 'I came to tell you that it'll be over in a couple of hours.'

Her eyes widened. 'How do you know?'

'I've just heard on the radio. The eye passed over the coast about seventy miles south an hour ago. It's still heading in the same direction—away from us— and once they get over land cyclones invariably weaken.'

'Thank heavens.' She smiled palely. 'I hate to think what it would have been like in the thick of it.'

'Yes—look, why don't you have a break? I'll look after Jess.'

'What about the house?'

'Milly's mopping up, but there's not much more we can do until it stops raining. There's no great damage.'

'All right. Just for an hour, if you don't mind,' she said quietly.

'Take an aspirin and lie down—take as long as you want.' He turned back to Jess.

She did, and although she hadn't planned to fall asleep she did just that. When she woke the sun was shining, the wind had dropped and the rain had stopped.

It was like a miracle, she thought as she stared out of her window. The sun was actually setting in a blaze of fiery splendour—and the roof of Raefe's beach shelter was sitting in a huge puddle in the middle of the lawn. A tinge of amusement lit her eyes as she thought of all the work he'd put in to the hut, and then she wondered why she should find anything amusing that was to do with Raefe Stevensen.

Still, at least her headache had gone. She had a shower and washed her hair, changed into fresh clothes and, with a deep breath, sallied forth. But Raefe was down at the stockyards, she discovered, as were all the men of the property—and Jess was sitting on Milly's lap in the playroom, introducing her to her 'family'.

Francesca paused on the doorstep and thought, with a strange, tearing little ache, I should be *happy*. Happy for Jess and happy for myself, because the sooner I can get away the better...

She drove Milly home just before it got dark—the older woman was obviously tired—and Raefe came up in time to have dinner with them before Jess went to bed. He was obviously tired too, but they maintained a stream of conversation for Jess's benefit. What Francesca refused to do was so much as catch his eye.

Then Jess went to bed and they were alone. Raefe stretched and yawned.

'Why don't you go to bed too?' Francesca murmured. 'It's been a big day.'

'Mmm...how's your headache?'

'How did you—?' She stopped. She was drying the dishes, half turned away from him—he was sitting at the kitchen table with his hands behind his head.

'I could see the pain in your eyes—I had one myself, anyway.'

'Oh.' She dried the last plate, then picked up a pile of them and put them away in a cupboard. 'It's fine now, thanks. And I must tell you—' she turned and their eyes met at last '—I think Jess is going to take to Milly. I was a bit worried yesterday—she seemed to have gone into her shell—but this afternoon she was much better.'

'So?'

'So I can go soon,' she said, after an age during which their gazes clashed and all that was unsaid between them hung in the air like a twirled and tormented thread.

'About last night,' he said abruptly. 'I—'

'I don't want to talk about it. I just want to go—as soon as possible,' Francesca said quietly.

'I... Have you rung your father?'

'No. If I go in the next couple of days I won't need to.'

Raefe frowned. 'He may just have heard about the cyclone.'

'Then he can ring me.'

'Are you seriously being groomed to take over?' he asked after a moment.

'Other than simply being humoured?' Francesca said, with a glimmer of amusement that died almost before it was born. 'Is that what you mean?'

He shrugged.

She leant back against the counter and folded her arms. 'Probably being humoured,' she commented prosaically, then added with some irony, 'I...insisted that I should know more about this empire he flourishes at me all the time. So he said, "Go ahead, dear girl, go ahead."' She raised her eyebrows. 'As if to say, I'm sure this phase will *pass*, kind of thing. So I went ahead.'

'Determined to prove him wrong—is that how you came to be at Wirra?'

'Well, I hadn't planned on Wirra. He suggested that when—' She stopped and glanced at Raefe wryly.

'The married man?'

Francesca started to say something, then paused. 'What exactly did you hear?'

'That you'd been banished up to Wirra because of an affair with a married man.'

Their eyes met. 'There was no affair,' she said quietly.

'So what did happen?'

'He was on the board of one of the Valentine companies I was getting to know. He started to send me flowers and gifts, all of which I returned—as well as doing my level best to keep him at arm's length in a businesslike way. But unfortunately his wife found out about the flowers, and she confronted me one day in a very public place.

'I'm not sure what infuriated her more—her husband's perfidy or the fact that I told her he was a disgusting little creep and I no more wanted him than I would want a hole in the head. It was at the company's annual dinner dance.'

Raefe was silent for a moment, then he burst out laughing.

Francesca didn't follow suit. She said instead, with a touch of bleakness, 'I'm glad you find it amusing. As a matter of fact so did my father.'

'You didn't slap his face? The husband?'

'I'm only sorry I didn't,' she said ruefully. 'But I was trying to be very adult, mature and businesslike. I was trying to prove, if you must know, that I might be capable of stepping into my father's shoes if ever the need should arise. He said, my father, "Chessie, you really don't need to bother your head about the empire, dear girl! Especially if it's going to land you in this kind of bother."'

'Very galling?' Raefe suggested.

'Extremely.'

'But you didn't stay to fight it out? Or at least fight

for your right to be considered adult, mature and businesslike?'

Francesca looked into the middle distance, then sighed. 'I poured a glass of wine over him—the husband. In the heat of the moment. But, anyway—' she grimaced '—I ended up feeling rather sorry for the poor woman, so when Dad said it was a kind of no-win situation, and suggested Wirra if I was still determined to persevere, I—it seemed like a good idea at the time. I might have known it would all get horribly distorted, though.'

'You're a...strange mixture, Chessie,' Raefe said slowly.

'Don't tell me. I know,' she returned wearily.

'I mean, sometimes you are mature and adult and it's not all that difficult to imagine you as a cool, level-headed, businesswoman tycoon—is that really your ambition?'

'Perhaps,' she said guardedly, her eyes downcast.

He waited, watching her speculatively, as if he thought there might be more.

'Did you have *your* life mapped out to the last detail at twenty-three?' she said, lifting her lashes suddenly.

'No...'

She was silent.

'Would I be wrong in assuming you don't totally despise your father?' he said then.

Francesca moved abruptly. 'Yes.'

'I wonder—there's a lot of him in you.'

'Again, you don't have to tell me that. But it so happens I'm also quite unlike him in many respects, as you might have discovered if you hadn't been so determined to believe I was tarred with the same brush.'

'I've told you, I don't—now.'

She glanced at him almost absently, and it occurred to Raefe that she'd fined down a little in the last few days. The heat, all the extra work she'd taken on, the cyclone and, just possibly, what he himself had done to her had stripped some of that expensive gloss from Chessie Valentine. And, damnably, he found himself thinking that this fined-down version carried as much allure if not more than the previous one.

Because it showed her character? he pondered. Because she was still lovely—even when she was tired, pale and a little thinner, when her head was pounding but she carried on, when you knew there was a lot more to her than you'd imagined, knew she was brave, feisty and sometimes a complete enigma?

'What am I going to do with you, Chessie?' he murmured, barely audibly and without thinking—without realising he was thinking aloud, in fact.

'Do?' He'd known it would happen, and it did as she repeated the word. Her spine straightened, her shoulders squared and that gorgeous mouth he'd plundered so pleasurably a few times now set severely for a moment. 'Just go to bed, Raefe; there's nothing you need to do,' she said evenly. 'Didn't I tell you? You don't need to lose any sleep over me.' And she got up and strode out of the kitchen.

He waited until he heard her bedroom door close, then got up himself and went into the lounge to stand staring down at the photo of himself and Olivia.

Although she had closed herself into her bedroom Francesca wasn't ready for bed, and she sat by the window for a long time, looking at the moonlit garden, watching the shadows float over the sea as clouds sailed across the moon, remembering the sound of the wind although it was now a still, perfect night.

Rather like the shadows that exist between me and Raefe, she thought tiredly, although now it was more a mental weariness. It's almost as if there's a dark moon up there, making sure any hopes I have are doomed—why do I persist in having any hopes?

Because there are times, she answered herself, when you can't forget what it feels like to be in his arms, times when it feels so natural just to talk to him, times when you see how he cares for his daughter, his sister, his staff… But of course that's also the crux of it. How much he still cares for his wife.

She laid her head on her arms suddenly, and closed her eyes.

They cleaned up the next day.

Pete and Raefe spent most of the day down at the cattle yards, and, between them, Francesca and Milly dragged anything that was faintly damp out into the sunshine and mopped and polished the rest.

Then Francesca armed herself with a pair of secateurs, a rake and a straw broom, and attacked the battered bougainvillea and all the shrubs and small trees in the garden, pruning them back to some sort of shape and piling all the broken branches into a heap with the intention of burning it as soon as it dried out sufficiently.

Milly remonstrated with her once, telling her she was doing too much, and out in the glare of the sun too! But she soldiered on until about four o'clock, when all of a sudden the world tilted alarmingly and she fell over onto the grass. Milly and Jess ran out anxiously.

'I told you—I told her,' Francesca heard Milly say to someone else, and realised with an inward groan that Raefe had arrived on the scene. 'You've got to take things easy in this heat—I told her.'

Whereupon she was swung up in a pair of strong arms and Raefe was saying unemotionally, 'There are times when you can't tell her anything.'

But that was mild compared to what he said to her after carrying her inside, laying her down on her bed and pointedly closing the bedroom door on Jess, Milly and Pete.

Francesca opened her eyes cautiously and discovered that the world was no longer spinning like a top. 'Thank heavens,' she whispered, and tried to sit up.

She was thrust back. 'Don't be a bloody fool,' Raefe said savagely, and continued, 'What the hell did you think you were doing? Surely you know better by now?'

'I...' Francesca licked her lips. 'Well, I put sunscreen on and I wore a hat—'

'But you obviously neglected to drink copiously— What's the hurry, anyway?' he added scathingly.

Tears pricked at the back of Francesca's eyes because that was something she'd asked herself during the day, but she had been unable to come up with the answer. It struck her now, as she stared up into Raefe's angry eyes, that she'd been motivated by an obscure desire to leave Bramble as she'd found it, serene, lovely and a bit like paradise—because she had to go, and go very soon.

She closed her eyes on the tears and by a huge effort of will banished them. 'I don't know,' she said with a shrug and a forcibly summoned up tinge of amusement. 'Once I got going it was hard to stop. I'll be fine.' She did sit up this time. 'Don't worry.' And she started to swing her legs off the bed.

'Lie back,' he commanded grimly. 'You'll just stay there and do as you're told.' And he strode to the door, issued some orders down the passage and returned eventually with a large glass of cloudy liquid. 'Drink it.'

She swallowed. 'What is it?'

'An electrolyte solution to replace all the mineral salts you've lost. What do you think it is—arsenic?' He put the glass into her hands.

'I wouldn't be surprised,' she murmured, and, turning away from him, drank it down slowly. Then she handed him the glass and lay back with a sigh, closing her eyes again.

'How do you feel now?' she heard him say, in slightly less aggravated tones.

'OK.'

'Then just rest there; we'll bring your dinner to you.'

'Yes, *sir*.'

'Francesca...' he said dangerously.

She opened her eyes indignantly. 'Will you go away, Raefe? I feel enough of a fool as it is—you don't have to rub it in.'

'I'm not; I'm merely trying to find out exactly how you are feeling now.'

She sat up abruptly and said bitterly, 'I've just told you—like an utter idiot. Isn't that enough—what more do you want?'

'Chessie?'

They both turned to see Jess standing at the door.

'Are you all right, Chessie?' Jess advanced into the room, anxiety written clearly on her little face and her two monkeys in her arms.

'Yes, sugar, I'm—I just got a bit hot. I'll be fine.'

'She's going to rest for a bit, Jess,' Raefe said abruptly.

'Then I'll leave you Mo and Flo so you won't be lonely, Chessie,' Jess said in a soothing tone. But she did more. She climbed onto the bed, hugged Francesca, arranged Mo and Flo on the pillow then climbed off and took Raefe by the hand. 'Shall we leave her in peace?'

Their gazes caught over Jess's head, Raefe's and Francesca's, and it was obvious his daughter had discomfited him somewhat. But he had the grace to look rueful as he said gravely, 'Of course. You're right, Jess. My apologies, Chessie.' He ushered Jess out and closed the door softly.

Francesca gathered Mo and Flo into her arms and found herself weeping into their fur.

Milly brought her dinner and reassured herself that there was nothing wrong with the patient that a good sleep and plenty of liquid wouldn't cure. She also confided that Raefe had put Jess to bed and that she herself would be sleeping next door to Jess, so that Francesca wouldn't have to worry if she woke.

Francesca got up after she'd eaten and had a shower. But she found herself feeling strangely lethargic, so she changed into her nightwear and got properly into bed. The house was quiet, and she was lying quietly, half asleep, when Raefe walked in.

She blinked, sat up and looked at him enquiringly.

'It's your father,' he said, and she saw that he had the portable phone in his hand. 'He did hear about the cyclone—belatedly. Are you up to talking to him?'

Francesca sighed inwardly. 'Yes. I might as well get it over with.' She took the phone, and Raefe hesitated, then walked out.

She took a deep breath. 'Hi, Dad,' she said brightly into the instrument. 'If you're worried I've been blown away, I'm still in one piece!'

'And you didn't think to let me know you were all right,' her father barked down the line. 'For crying out loud, Chessie—I didn't even know there'd been a cyclone until…someone suggested that it might be an idea to check up on you a few minutes ago!'

'Well, there you go—only a few minutes of panic, which was probably better than me trying to contact you at the heart of the mayhem because there wouldn't have been anything you could have done anyway, you see,' she said reasonably.

'Don't take that tone with me, Chessie,' he growled. 'What you don't know is that in two days' time I was coming to get you myself— Look, what the hell are you doing up in that God-forsaken spot anyway? I want you *home*—'

'Dad, you know you can't order me around any longer,' she broke in. 'I'll come when I'm good and ready.'

There was a short silence, then her father spoke in an entirely different tone. 'Chessie, there's something I have to tell you. My dear…'

It must have been ten minutes after the call ended that Raefe came back. He stopped in the doorway, then swore softly and closed the door. He came over to the bed and stared down at her as she lay with her face buried, her shoulders shaking and the muffled sound of awful grief coming from the pillow.

'Chessie?' He sat down on the bed and touched her tentatively, then, when she stiffened, he gathered her into his arms, turning her over and smoothing some strands of hair from her hot, wet face as tears streamed ceaselessly down her cheeks. 'What is it?' he said, rocking her as he might have rocked Jess. 'Tell me, Chessie.'

'He's…' She gulped and tried again. 'He's g-getting m-married!'

CHAPTER NINE

'IS THAT such a disaster?' he said after a moment, still rocking her as she wept against his shoulder. 'I mean, is it someone you hate, or think he shouldn't be marrying?'

'I don't even know her. I've never laid eyes on her,' Francesca sobbed. 'But she's different, he says. She's older than the usual...ones. She's thirty-seven and...and—'

'Well, if he's—what?—fifty-two or so, it's just as well.'

'And she's not after his money because she's a widow with plenty of money herself, and she's a career woman,' Francesca went on heedlessly, taking deep, shuddering breaths.

'But that's got to be a plus, Chessie,' he pointed out.

'You don't understand!' Francesca pulled herself away and glared up at him. 'He's finally fallen in love again. Properly. She's having his baby!'

'I'm sure...' Raefe paused '...you'll never be overlooked in any way—financially or—'

'Do you *really* think I care about that?' Her wet blue eyes could still smoulder with anger, he discovered, and she ground her teeth. 'Don't you see? They'll be a *family* and I'll be hovering on the fringes as I've always done. The daughter he sent away to boarding-school and finishing school and anywhere he could send me.

'He said…he tried to tell me how much he regretted all that, how he hoped to be able to make amends now. He even said that *she'd* reformed him—I'll believe that when I see it. But why couldn't he have reformed himself for *me*?' she said fiercely.

Raefe closed his eyes briefly and pulled her back into his arms. And after some minutes, when she'd visibly made a terrible effort to control herself and was lying desolate, drained and silent in his arms, he stroked her face and murmured, 'Not the perfect end to an imperfect day.'

She didn't respond.

'Have you made any plans, Chessie?'

'Plans to go home for the wedding—or just to go away from here?' she said huskily after an age, then shrugged. 'Yes, as a matter of fact. Tomorrow. At least I can tell Jess honestly that I've been called home urgently.'

'But will you go home?'

'Why not?' she said listlessly. 'I might as well get it over and done with. I don't suppose he'll give me a moment's peace until I do. But after that…' She trailed off.

He said something under his breath, and she struggled to sit up and said wryly, although with a give-away catch in her voice that she couldn't quite control, 'I keep telling you this—you don't have to lose any sleep over it, Raefe. So—'

'And you think that's possible, Chessie?' he interrupted quietly.

'I... Well...' Tears started afresh in her eyes.

'Because I don't. I certainly can't let you go on feeling like this.' And he bent his head and started to kiss her eyelids.

'That's not fair,' she whispered after an age, when she'd been thoroughly kissed. 'I can't—I don't seem to have the strength to fight my way out of a paper bag at the moment...'

'Why fight it?' he said softly, and slid the narrow strap of her blue camisole top off her shoulder. 'We're two people in a certain amount of need, and we're two people who have forged a lot of respect for each other—at least I have for you.' He lowered his mouth to the satiny hollow at the base of her throat.

'But, Raefe, there's something I should—'

'You should...?' He raised his grey eyes to hers. 'Chessie, if you really don't want this, tell me now, before it's too late. I may not be able to stop again.'

'I...' She licked her lips and felt his fingers lying just lightly on the curve of her shoulder. She was achingly conscious of both the sense of protection and the wonderful feeling of being in his arms, of the warmth and strength she'd felt once before, the rapture that came to her just at lying against him—and the promise of exquisite pleasure to come.

I've resisted it for so long, she thought, but this is the first time I've wanted it with my heart and soul and every fibre of me; this is the first man who has made me feel this way—why not take this moment, even if I don't know where it can lead? At least I love him, even if he doesn't love me. At least I can have the memories...

'Chessie—?'

'No, Raefe,' she whispered, and buried her face in his shoulder briefly. 'I do want it. Could you—just hold me for a moment, please?'

And she couldn't doubt the urgent need in him as he held her close in the moments before he laid her back on the bed and lay down beside her.

'I always knew they'd be like this.'

'Did you? Like what?'

'Like perfect, full, exquisite fruit, Chessie,' he murmured.

She was sitting on her heels on the bed between his legs, facing him, and he'd slipped her camisole top off and was gazing at her breasts. He slid his hands round her slender waist and she raised her arms to put hers on his shoulders.

He watched with downcast lids as she moved her hands again and her breasts moved too, then he looked up into her eyes. 'They have been on my mind since the day I first saw you. They— It would be fair to say they haven't given me a minute's peace since the time they appeared before my eyes in a violet bikini-top, then under a yellow swimsuit and so on.' He brought his hands round and cupped their rose-tipped fullness.

Francesca breathed a little raggedly. 'Would it have helped if I'd never worn the bikini?'

He shook his head and his eyes were wry. 'No.'

Her lips curved and she leant forward slightly to kiss him on the brow.

'Moreover,' he continued, and stroked her nipples, 'they weren't the only problem.'

'No?' she breathed, and trembled as his touch on

her nipples caused a wave of sensation to flow down her body.

'No—oh, no.' He moved his hands back to her waist, lifted her so she was resting on her knees, then slid them beneath her silky blue sleep-shorts. 'These too.' He spread his fingers around her buttocks. 'And your legs. All—very problematical.'

'Can I tell you what I like about you?' She linked her hands around his neck and looked down at him, her eyes wide.

'Go ahead.'

'Your eyes and your hands,' she said with a perfectly straight face, but in the blue depths of her eyes there was a teasing little glint.

'Is that so?' His lips twisted. 'These hands?' And he used them to slide her shorts down to her knees.

Her lips parted as his fingers wandered back up the front of her thighs to touch her lightly and most intimately, while the other hand returned to her breasts. 'You're... Remind me not to tease you again, Raefe—that's almost unbearably lovely,' she said honestly, and caught her bottom lip between her teeth as her whole body rippled with pleasure.

'Chessie...' He said her name then took her in his arms and rolled them both over so they were lying side by side. '*You're* almost unbearably lovely,' he added as he dealt with his own clothes then came back to her, and she caught her breath in another kind of pleasure because he was lean and strong and golden...

What followed developed a rhythm as if they were both of one mind, one force. But, although she knew his need and hers were mounting swiftly, he didn't allow himself to rush. Consequently, when the moment came she faltered only briefly, a bare second, then was overtaken once more by all the feelings of joy and desire he'd aroused in her.

She gave herself up to the ultimate sensation that claimed them together with such heart-stopping delight that it was left to Raefe to bring her back to earth, and she clung to him with the intensity of someone who'd been transported to another planet.

Then she thanked him with tears in her eyes, and fell asleep in his arms moments later.

He stared down at the spread of her hair on the pillow and the twisted grace and glory of her body beside his in the lamplight. Her mouth was set softly, her lashes casting shadows on the faint blue marks of exhaustion printed below her eyes. He stared down at her with his mind still reeling in the moment before he leant over and switched off the bedside lamp.

He drew the sheet up, put one arm behind his head, with the other still cradling her to his side, and stared at the darkened ceiling with the missing piece of the puzzle now firmly in place. Was that what she'd been going to tell him? That Francesca Valentine had contrived, against all probability, to remain a virgin? He closed his eyes abruptly.

Francesca woke slowly. The lamp was on again. It was dark outside but the first faint pre-dawn stirring of the birds could be heard. Raefe was sitting on the side of the bed with his trousers on, buttoning up his shirt.

'Oh…' she whispered. She was covered by the sheet but naked beneath it, and a look of frowning wariness came to her eyes that caused him, against all expectations, to smile.

'Why?' he asked, with that smile still playing on his lips.

'Why...what?'

'Are you looking like that?'

'I'm not sure how I'm looking.'

'As if you're about to be extremely exasperated with yourself.'

'Oh, that—I...it happens from time to time that I wake up with the feeling that I've done something rather...unwise the day before—a presentiment of doom and gloom. And invariably I'm right—it just takes a moment or two to remember—' She broke off and sat up urgently, clutching the sheet about her.

'Chessie...' He paused and cupped her cheek. 'Whatever it was, wise or otherwise, you did it beautifully. But I wish you'd told me.' His grey eyes were suddenly sombre.

'I...' Her voice got caught in her throat. 'I mean—could you tell? How—?'

'Yes, I could tell.'

'But it didn't make it any worse— What I mean is, it didn't seem to flaw it in any way. Not for me, that is...' Her voice died away.

'No, it didn't do that.' His fingers moved on her cheek then slid through her hair. 'It was wonderful.'

'So?' she whispered, and swallowed as sudden understanding came to her. 'Now you think you have to—but you don't. I only— That *wasn't* why I did it.'

'I believe you. And that's not why I'll be marrying you either, Chessie,' he said steadily, and ignored the way her breath jolted. 'I'd only rather have known in case I hurt you. But I'll be marrying you because you're beautiful, you're brave—you're all the things I didn't think you were. You see, you've routed me completely.' He leant forward and brushed his lips against hers. 'Besides which, I don't think I can live without you.'

'But...'

'Chessie, there are people stranded in a farmhouse about a hundred miles west of here—I happened to intercept their call on the radio when I got up a bit earlier. They've got no power, other than a fading battery for the radio, and a baby who is sick. I need to go now, but I'll be back as soon as I can and we can discuss it all then.

'Go back to sleep. Sweet dreams,' he added, kissing her properly this time and laying her back against the pillows. Then he got up, switched off the lamp and walked out, closing the door softly.

'Jess,' Francesca said while they ate the breakfast that Milly had cooked for them. 'Jess, my father rang me last night. He—um—was really worried about the cyclone.'

'I didn't know you had a father,' Jess said interestedly. 'Is he like mine?'

'No. That is, because I'm much older than you, *he's* much older...'

She paused, thinking that she'd known this would be difficult but that it was going to exceed even her expectations. Then there was the sound of a vehicle pulling up outside, and within moments Sarah swept into the kitchen, followed by a man.

'But I thought you were in Tahiti,' Francesca said, rising dazedly.

'Tahiti can wait—can't it, Mark?' She pulled the man forward by his hand and put it into Chessie's. 'Say how do you do, you two. I've told Mark all about you—and as soon as I heard about the cyclone I knew you'd need help! I didn't even bother to let Raefe know we were coming in case he tried to dissuade me.

'Darling!' She swept Jess up. 'What exciting times you've been having! And have I got some lovely new clothes for you!'

'Er—there wouldn't be a cup of coffee around?' Mark Ellery said plaintively as he shook Francesca's hand, and his humorous, nice brown eyes rested on her. 'We've been driving all night virtually, but you look as if you could do with one too!'

'But why didn't you tell me about the Forsters—why didn't Raefe?'

They were seated at the breakfast table and Milly had tactfully removed herself and Jess.

'We didn't want to do anything to… You were so happy, and we were so happy for you,' Francesca said.

Mark and Sarah looked at each other ruefully, but their love for each other was obvious.

Francesca sipped some coffee and took a breath. 'Actually, you couldn't have come at a better time— for me, that is. I was just trying to explain it all to Jess, but I wouldn't have been happy about leaving her with Milly—although I think they're going to get on really well. The thing is, I've been ordered home. My father is getting married in a couple of days' time.'

Sarah blinked. 'Where *is* Raefe? Does he know this?'

Francesca explained. 'I'd almost made up my mind to stay until he got back, but with you here now... And,' she said slowly, 'it might be the best time to go—when Jess is excited, happy and distracted.'

She waited anxiously as she saw Sarah digest this, and didn't realise her eyes were unconsciously pleading.

'But,' Sarah said slowly, 'you will keep in touch, won't you, Chessie? You're like part of the family now.'

'Yes...'

On the difficult six-hour drive from Bramble that morning—supposedly six hours, but becoming much longer as she had to make several detours to avoid flooded roads—Francesca had plenty of time to reflect that she'd only told a couple of lies—in fact the same lie but to different people.

She'd promised both Jess and Sarah that she would never lose touch. Jess will forget, she consoled herself. But each time she thought this she bit her lip at the memory of Jess's disappointed little face and the tears in her eyes.

As for Raefe—would he forget? Would he be relieved? She swallowed. She'd thought of leaving a note for him, but what could she say? Thanks for the memories? It was wonderful, but marrying me was not something you intended to do until you found out I was a virgin? Thanks all the same but I don't think that's the most important benchmark between us—because, while it might indicate to you that I'm more worthy than you'd imagined, it doesn't lay to rest the ghost of Olivia...?

She got to Cairns just before dark and found the car dealership where she'd bought her four-wheel drive mercifully still open. She left it with them to sell for her, and by the skin of her teeth caught the last flight out. This took her to Sydney, not Melbourne, her home town, but it was so late by then she booked into a hotel and went straight to bed.

The next day she didn't leave the hotel, although she did leave a message for her father that morning to the effect that she was on her way home—the wedding was in five days' time, slightly further ahead than she'd given Sarah to understand, so perhaps that was another lie, she thought miserably.

If he's so adamant I should be there, why didn't he tell me sooner, or why can't he delay it? she wondered—and sneezed.

Two hours later, her nose was running, her head throbbing, her throat aching and her limbs almost too painful to move, but she did make the effort to lift the phone and call for the house doctor.

A severe cold, he proclaimed, and when she protested that she'd just come from a part of the country where it was almost impossible to get a cold he advised her that you could get colds anywhere. Changes of climate, air-conditioning and so on could make you more vulnerable.

He prescribed bed-rest for at least two days and departed with the observation that she might have been a bit run-down to start with. She rang her father again late that afternoon.

'Where the devil are you, Chessie?'

She explained, although she didn't give him exact details.

'I'm coming to get you myself, right now,' he barked down the phone. 'Tell me exactly where you are.'

'Dad—' she blew her nose and mopped her streaming eyes '—if you love me at all, just leave me in peace,' she said thickly.

'But I really wanted you to have a chance to get to know Mary before the wedding,' he said frustratedly.

'Then you left it a bit late,' she commented drily.

'Chessie...' He heaved an audible sigh down the line. 'You have no idea how difficult this has been to tell you. We've been at such loggerheads since you grew up, for which I take all the blame, my dear, and anyway, you haven't been exactly easy to lay hands on lately. By the way, who is this Raefe Stevensen?'

'Why?' she asked warily. 'Has he been in touch?'

'Not since he rang me to tell me where you were— and to tell me a few other things. He was damned insolent, if you must know,' said her father, sounding more like his old self.

Francesca relaxed a bit, but avoided the question. 'Dad, I give you my word. I'll be home in time for the wedding.'

He hesitated. 'Won't you at least tell me where you are?'

It was her turn to hesitate, then she relented and they chatted for a few minutes more. Her parting words were, 'I'll be home.'

Three hours later there was a knock on her door

which, when she opened it, revealed her father and a strange woman. And that was how she came to be transported home in her father's private jet that same night.

And how, five days later, she dressed to attend his wedding ceremony in a more positive frame of mind about it than she'd dreamt possible.

She took the time to ponder it all in her own room in the lovely Toorak mansion she'd grown up in.

In a bid to hide the last effects of her cold, on top of a month in the tropics, she'd had a masseuse come to the house that morning—a woman who had soothed and anointed her body with a gentle massage and had given her a manicure and a facial.

It had been during this that she had thought of how her father had changed. And it was Mary Wilson, soon to be Valentine, who was not beautiful but elegant, poised, wealthy in her own right and possessed of a very sharp brain—she was a barrister—who had achieved it.

She was also, once you got to know her, warm, witty and wise. And it was very clear, despite faint glimpses of vulnerability about being pregnant for the first time at thirty-seven, that this woman had only one reason for marrying Frank Valentine—she loved him. And she'd contrived, somehow, or other, to win over his daughter too…

So, Francesca thought now as she put on a Thai silk suit the colour of wild rice with a short skirt and ivory accessories, it's worked out well for several people— Dad and Mary, Sarah and Mark. And Raefe?

She stared at her reflection. Mary's hairdresser had

also called earlier, and had swept her hair back into an elegant pleat. She wore pearls in her ears and about her throat—a set that had belonged to her mother. But it was impossible to think about Raefe—who had made no move to get in touch with her—without having a sense of that dark moon she'd imagined once, clouding her day, her very being.

It'll pass, she told herself. You were the one who thought you could make do with memories. You were the one who knew about Olivia.

It was a small, lovely old church where the morning ceremony was to be conducted, with the reception to be held at home. In order to keep the Press at bay, numbers had been strictly limited, and there was discreet but nevertheless thorough surveillance of the guests as they arrived at the church. No one unrecognised or without an invitation would be admitted.

Francesca was ushered to the front pew, and she sat down. There were to be no bridesmaids, groomsmen or attendants.

Then someone sat down beside her—a man in a dark suit, a tall man with fair hair and grey eyes, although she'd never seen him so formally dressed...

'You!' she gasped.

'Yes, Chessie,' Raefe agreed.

'But how did you get in?' she whispered. 'No one—'

'I was invited.'

'*Invited?* But how? Why? I don't understand.' Although it was all said *sotto voce*, there was no mistaking her confusion and anger.

His grey eyes rested on her with all his old amusement mirrored in them—plus something else. 'We thought you mightn't make a scene here, Chessie. You look stunning, by the way.'

'I ''mightn't make a scene''?' she repeated, almost soundlessly. 'Oh!'

But then the organ swelled, the congregation rose and her father walked down the aisle with his wife-to-be on his arm.

CHAPTER TEN

'I SUPPOSE you've been invited to the reception too,'
Francesca said in a bitter undertone as Raefe walked
with her down the aisle behind her father and Mary at
the end of the short service.

It had been an unnerving experience—kneeling beside him, praying beside him with her perfumed body
aquiver beneath the silk suit, with all her perfect
grooming hiding—she hoped—the helpless seething
of emotions, with the touch of his hand on her elbow
evoking all sorts of memories.

'Your father said that so long as you were there for
the toasts we could do as we liked. I gather it's only
to be a short reception anyway.'

This was true, but she didn't have much time to
think about it because as they stepped out of the
church it was obvious the Press had been alerted by
someone, and they were there in force.

Frank Valentine grimaced, but granted them five
minutes. He also insisted his daughter Francesca was
included in the photos, and it was inevitable, as Raefe
got into the second limousine with Francesca, that he
was photographed too. Several members of the press
corps called out, asking his name.

'Well, now *you'll* be in the social pages,' Francesca
said tartly as they were driven away.

He took her hand. She resisted briefly but he

wouldn't let it go, so she let it lie in his and turned her head to look out of the window. 'So I will,' he said wryly. '"The mystery man"—but I'll be the one you marry, did they but know it.'

'Look, Raefe—' her tone was taut '—you can't expect me to fight this out with you today. It's my father's wedding day!'

'I'm pleased to hear it, Chessie. I didn't come to fight you.'

She made a frustrated little sound.

'I'm also pleased to hear,' he went on quietly, linking his fingers through hers, 'that his marriage now has your approval.'

'You...' She turned her head to look at him, her eyes an incredulous deep blue. 'How long have you and my father been in cahoots?'

'A few days. Jess sends her love.'

Her lips parted and their eyes locked. 'How could you?' she whispered.

'I'll tell you that later—we're here.'

She blinked away some foolish tears as the car swept into the forecourt of the house, and took a deep breath.

There were more photos as they alighted, this time official ones, and although Raefe discreetly stayed out of the limelight this time he was never far away in the main lounge, where the reception was set up and the guests mingled.

'Dad,' she managed to say, 'why did you do this?'

'Chessie, he came to see me and lay his case before me the day after I got you home. I thought he might just be the one for you, my dear, dear girl, but I insisted that you have a few days—not only to get over your cold but also to have things out with yourself.

'Send him away if you wish, but I'd think twice about it if I were you. I may not have been much of a father but it's my dearest wish to see you happy, and if nothing else he's proved to me he has your best interests at heart— Senator Mitchell! Great to see you—have you met my daughter Francesca?'

She responded mechanically, thinking drily at the same time that some things about her father would never change. And that was how it continued throughout the toasts and the cutting of the cake. Then the bridal couple departed in showers of confetti and rose petals—they were off to Fiji—and the guests started to trickle away. Until there were only the two of them left—and the staff.

'A glass of champagne, Chessie?'

'More setting of the scene, Raefe?' she said with irony. 'Did you really think doing this in the middle of a wedding would make me feel all soft and sentimental? Make me change my mind?'

'No, although that may have been your father's motivation. But mine is quite different. This is the first opportunity I've been granted to tell you about all the things I've done wrong.'

She accepted the glass he was offering her and took a sip. Then her shoulders slumped and she said huskily, 'It's not your fault—none of it is. Once I knew, that's when I should have left. Come to that, I should never have gone to Bramble in the first place. Sorry…'

'If you'd never come, Chessie,' he said slowly, his eyes holding her tear-filled ones, 'my life would have been poorer and my perceptions duller, and, what's worse, I might never have been able to pay Olivia the final compliment.'

Her eyes widened. 'What…what do you mean?'

He took her hand. 'Is there somewhere a bit more private we could go, Chessie?'

She looked around dazedly, and was surprised to see someone operating a vacuum cleaner not far from them.

'Yes.' She cleared her throat, then led the way through the house to a glass-fronted conservatory overlooking the garden at the rear. There were comfortable settees and chairs set amongst the potted plants, statues and hanging baskets, and it was always peaceful.

Francesca hesitated, then sat in a single armchair. Raefe sat down opposite, putting a silver bucket holding the champagne bottle down at his feet.

'How…how is Jess?' she blurted out—something she'd been willing herself not to ask.

'Chessie…' He paused, his fair head bent as he studied his glass, then he raised sombre grey eyes to hers. 'This has got nothing to do with Jess. Nor has it anything to do with you being a virgin—although I admit that you took me by surprise there.'

'I know,' she whispered. 'I also know you wouldn't have asked me to marry you otherwise, although you denied it, but it had to have something to do with it. And, you see—'

'I see that I hurt you badly,' he broke in. 'It was as if I was saying that was the only test that mattered to me—it wasn't that. But, yes, I accept the charge that at the time it was, or so I *told* myself, a reason to ask you to marry me.

'It was only that night, when I got home to discover you'd left, that I was honest enough to admit to myself that I was using it as an excuse. Using it to excuse the fact that I'd fallen in love with another woman when I'd thought that not only *couldn't* it happen to me, but that it *shouldn't.*'

Francesca discovered suddenly that she was afraid to breathe.

'Then I worked out why you'd left,' he went on. 'Because you'd seen through it all. And I knew what a fool I'd been. I saw, at last, that Olivia was gone from me for ever but would always live on in Jess. And I knew that her memory deserved better.

'Those times we had, the good marriage, the things I learnt, deserved better than to be locked away in bitterness and a lifetime of regret; they deserved the final compliment of being able to go forward again, able to live and love again.

'But most of all I saw that I'd fallen in love with you, Chessie, and I was desperately afraid that I'd lost you because all of this had come clear to me too late.'

'Is...is this true?' Francesca stammered.

'Only too true. But there is one thing I may have overlooked.'

'What's that?'

He sat forward and clasped his hands. 'I kept telling myself that you had to be in love with me. And all that day, while I was ferrying people, sick babies, dogs and cats to safety, even though I was still deluding myself about my motives, I was sure of yours. I didn't think it was possible for you to be so affected—so beautifully joyful and ecstatic—by sensation alone unless it had something to do with me, warts and all,' he said, with a strange little smile.

Francesca closed her eyes and felt the colour pour into her cheeks. 'Did I...? I did go over the top, didn't I?' she said hollowly. 'It's something I've never been able to cure myself of.'

'Chessie,' he said very quietly, 'it's my heartfelt desire that you never change—in bed or out of it. But you haven't answered the question.'

'You haven't asked me—'

'Was I right in assuming you loved me?'

'Do you mean you...you came down here, won over my father, *told* me you were the one I was going to marry and so on, without knowing how I felt?'

'Well...' He paused and their eyes locked. 'I have no way of knowing it absolutely until *you* tell me, my darling Chessie.'

She trembled suddenly, put the back of her hand to her mouth and said indistinctly, 'Oh, Raefe...'

He stood up and drew her to her feet. 'Is it impossible to say?'

'No—it's just that I never thought my feelings could be returned. I mean, I hoped—but— Raefe, I may not make a very good wife—'

'Chessie, let's just take one thing at a time—do you love me?'

'*Yes*. Oh, yes...' But she was trembling and shaking and her eyes were anguished.

He put his arms around her. 'Thank heavens,' he said, barely audibly, as he held her very close, and she could hear his heart beating. 'So...' he held her away and looked into her eyes '...why are you so upset?'

'I don't know—it must be reaction. And—there are times when I'm terrible, I know. Times when I'm a Valentine through and through—times when you'll find me impossible, I'm sure, and—'

'Chessie, stop,' he said gently but firmly, and put a finger to her lips.

'But—'

'No. Relax.'

She took a deep breath, then laid her tear-stained cheek on his shoulder. 'I haven't been well—perhaps that's why I'm a bit emotional.'

He tilted her chin and smiled into her eyes—and all of a sudden she felt herself calming and starting to believe. He said, 'You were never terrible—you were unique.'

'Even when I all but—stripped?'

'Even then.'

'I thought you really hated me for that,' she said huskily.

'I tried to hate you. It didn't work.'

'You gave a pretty good imitation of it.'

'I can see I still have a lot to answer for,' he murmured wryly.

'No! *No*,' she repeated with a sudden glint of humour in her eyes. 'I don't believe in endless recriminations. I...just want to know that I can believe in this.'

'Chessie.' He looked down at her, and once again she was afraid to breathe because of what she saw in his eyes—the steady flame that told its own tale. 'I'm bereft without you. I'm haunted by you everywhere I turn. I have visions of you that give me no peace and no sleep. And most of all I loved you best, if that's possible, when the heat and the wear and tear of life at Bramble showed me a Chessie Valentine who was no longer a glossy golden girl but a brave, committed, still beautiful *woman* who would make the perfect partner for my soul as well as my body.'

'Raefe,' she whispered, 'you've just convinced me. You're the only man who's ever been interested in that side of me.'

'So...' His gaze lingered on her mouth, then he looked into her shining eyes. 'Will you marry me, Chessie?'

'Yes, please, Raefe. Yes, please...'

'We didn't have to do this,' she murmured about an hour later, when he'd booked them into a luxury hotel.

'Yes, we did. I want you on my own ground, not anyone else's.'

'So you're going to be one of those territorial husbands?' she teased.

'Very territorial,' he remarked, and began to undo the buttons of her jacket. He slid the silk off her shoulders and the jacket crumpled to the floor. 'As well as crazy about you. Would you let your hair down?'

She complied, laying the pins on the end of the bed, and shook her head so the toffee-coloured mass whirled then subsided.

'Mmm...' He made no move to touch her as she stood in her bra and skirt before him. 'It's just as well we were in a church when I first saw you again.'

'Is it?' she said softly.

'Oh, yes. Because even looking so…severely lovely as you were—'

'Was I?'

'Yes.' His lips twisted. 'With not a hair out of place, beautifully clothed and made up. Even—'

'Make-up,' Francesca said with a little imp of mischief dancing in her eyes. 'That reminds me—I didn't make myself up that night.'

His eyes narrowed. 'That night of the beach barbecue, when I accused you of…' He paused.

'Setting out to seduce you?' she suggested innocently. 'Yes, that night. It was Annette's idea—she wants to be a beautician as well as a hairdresser and she begged me to let her do my face. I must say she has absolute magic in her fingers, and—'

'I hesitate to interrupt you, Chessie,' he said, and folded his arms, looking at her with several emotions chasing through his eyes. 'But why couldn't you have just told me this at the time?'

'Ah, well, you see…' She paused and folded *her* arms. 'That's one of the problems I was talking about earlier. To do with being a Valentine. An inherent unwillingness, I'm afraid, to…well, to…'

'Lower oneself to explain *anything*?' he proffered.

'Something like that,' she agreed ruefully. 'But it wasn't entirely that.'

'No?'

'No,' she said gravely. 'There was a certain amount of gratification involved—at the fact that you *had* noticed.'

'So I remember—do you know what I had to do after you left me alone on the beach that night?'

'No.' She looked at him enquiringly.

'Go for a very long, strenuous swim, my dear Chessie. Which has happened to me twice now in our relationship.'

'Well—is there anything I can do to compensate for that?'

He was laughing as he reached for her, and it was warm and lovely as they laughed together and then quietened. And then he drew her down beside him on the bed, outlined her mouth with his finger, and bent his head to kiss her deeply.

Then they helped each other out of their clothes and made love until, for Francesca, that dark moon was replaced by star-shot splendour, and she could no longer doubt how much he loved her.

'How is Jess?' she asked a long time later, when they were still lying in each other's arms because it would have been unbearable to be parted.

'She'll be restored by this news,' he said quietly.

'I…' She trembled. 'If you only knew how hard it was to leave her.'

'I do.' He pushed his fingers through the tangle of her hair, smoothing it off her cheek. 'But I was the one who made you leave us. Will you come back, Chessie?'

'Of course. Will you—marry me first? Or should we break it to her gently?'

'I think we ought to marry each other as soon as possible.'

Her lips curved. 'That has a very equitable ring to it.'

'I'm glad you approve.' His grey eyes rested wryly

on her, then he pulled her close and buried his head in her hair. 'I love you.'

'You don't know what it does to me to hear you say so.' She ran her hand down the long muscles of his back.

He lifted his head abruptly. 'I'm not entirely sure what I've done to deserve you, Chessie.'

'Well, it's actually more than your eyes and your hands. It's—' She stopped, the smile dying in her eyes as she saw the intensity that had gripped him. 'It's quite simple. It seems to me that I was made for you, that's all.'

She felt him relax slowly and smiled lovingly into his eyes. 'You were saying something earlier—before I interrupted you—about it being just as well we were in a church?'

'So I was—it was just as well because otherwise I wouldn't have been able to keep my hands off you.'

She ran her hand through his hair, pushing it off his forehead. 'I quite like the thought of that.'

'Well, that's just as well too—because it's about to become an occupational hazard for you.'

'An occupational hazard?' she repeated, and chuckled. 'Just think—even my father will be eternally grateful to you, Raefe. No more discontented daughter storming about the place, trying to learn the ropes.'

'Ah, yes. I must tell you, though, that he warned me to make you happy—or else! In a very threatening manner.'

'Did he really?'

'Indeed he did, my darling Chessie. Nor was he the

only one—my own sister told me I was an absolute heel.'

'But I didn't—' Francesca stopped.

'Didn't you? Neither, I thought, did I,' he conceded ruefully. 'But the fact of the matter is she decided almost right from the beginning that we were right for each other. Tahiti was only ever an invention to keep us together.'

Francesca gasped, then nestled against him, laughing helplessly this time.

'So, in view of all this, may I take some steps along that path right now?' he asked.

'Make love to me again, you mean?'

'Only if it would make you happy.'

She raised her eyes to his, and they were a deep, adoring blue. 'You may.'